It's A Big World Out There

by Rex Crawford

Published by Flow Angel Media Publishing Group
est. 2020

It's A Big World Out There

First edition

ISBN: 978-1-960101-01-3

Some material in this novel are quotes taken from that of John Donne (1620), Leonardo Da Vinci and a poetry blog post from username 'Milkman' ref: www.originalpoetry.com/untitled-4_3 credit and recognition for these quotes remain for their original authors.

Table of Contents

Prologue

From the deepest, darkest corners of existence, there have been enemies lurking. They have been patient and cunning. They are able to anticipate all strategies of attack with the most unexpected defensive maneuvers with ease. This enemy knows man better than men know themselves. Mankind is on the verge of coming face to face with this greatest of all threats that has existed throughout history. This enemy has been closing in on the human race for centuries. They are the Cacodemons.

Off-world observers recognized the threat and devised a careful plan to help the people of Earth, so that they might be ready and have a fighting chance of defeating them. They are called Rapah, and they are strategically assigned to work with millions of key people on Earth, one-on-one. Their methods, though covert, are intended to give mankind the advantage that will be needed when the war begins in earnest. But time is running out, and the threat is ever-increasing.

It's A Big World Out There

by Rex Crawford

Chapter One:

The New Girl in Class

"Our fear of death is like our fear that summer will be short, but when we have had our swing of pleasure, our fill of fruit, and our swelter of heat, we say we have had our day." - John Donne, 1620

The summer had been short; it was September already. School began at the end of August, and after only two weeks, the fear and burden of not doing well had consumed the students of Ware Junior/Senior High.

It was Friday, September 7. Cameron was ready for the week to be over, even though it was just the second week of school, and it was going to be a short week because of Labor Day. He had gotten all his homework done last night, and even though he knew it wasn't done to perfection, he felt the relief of being able to turn something in. He didn't spend too much time on it because he had just gotten a new video game for his sixteenth birthday, and he just had to reach a respectable level before attending to anything else. Even with his mother's directive to get his room straightened up, along with cleaning the bathroom and taking out the trash, he felt that those chores could wait one more day. He did, however, get to his homework eventually, and that felt like quite an accomplishment for him on a Thursday night.

Cameron was tall for his age and well-proportioned despite being rather sedentary in his lifestyle. He had short, curly, dark brown hair that he hardly ever combed much since it always sat nicely up on top of his head. He lived in Ware, Massachusetts all his life and had friends that he would play video games with, but that was about the extent of his social life. The other kids at school would call them the "cave dwellers" because of their pale skin from being indoors much of the time.

He was a little early to school, so he took the long way through the multicolored hallways to the upper-class end of the school. He liked the journey through the earlier classes that he attended in his past. Not that it went back very far. He grew up in Ware and his past at Ware Junior/Senior High School was only the ninth and tenth grades. The halls were a dingy red for ninth, faded yellow for tenth, dark green for eleventh which was where he was, and bright blue for twelfth. When he reached his locker, there was no need to remember the combination since the handle was broken. He didn't mind as there was never anything of value that he left in it. Of all the lockers on the wall where his was, he had the only one that was broken.

When he arrived at home room that morning, his teacher, Mrs. Fletcher, introduced a new student—Sonja Olivetti. Cameron was instantly smitten. He had never felt this way before, and apparently, it showed. Bill and Kevin, his two closest friends, started laughing out loud as Cameron realized that his mouth and eyes were wide open, and he flushed red with embarrassment. She was tall and her shoulders served as cascades for her dark brown hair to flow over. She was also a bit more mature in places than most of the other girls in his class. Her family had just recently moved from Boston.

At lunch that day, Sonja was sitting at the last empty table. Bill and Kevin grabbed the last two seats at their table, forcing Cameron to have to sit across from Sonja.

"Awkward, right?" Cameron said to her as he sat down.

She looked at him and then at his lunch and then back at him.

"So, do you play baseball?" she said out of the blue.

Shocked that she would even speak to him, Cameron replied, "I play the video game version, so I know how to play, I mean the rules and things, but no, I don't play in real life."

"Real life, eh? What do you do in real life?" she replied.

"Well, I, you know, things, but I don't play sports," he said.

"What do you say we throw a ball around a little some time?" she asked. "You have to get up off your backside and get out there into the real world. The world is filled with questions that have to be answered."

"I guess I could do that. Do you know where the ball field is?" asked Cameron, before immediately adding, "Memorial Field, it's over by Family First Bank off South Street, but there's a field here at the school too."

"Yeah, it's not far from where I live in the Maple Street Annex, but we don't want to go there," Sonja replied.

"Wow, that means that you take the bus to school. That's a little too far to walk or bike," said Cameron.

"Well, sometimes my old man will be giving me a ride, I'm sure; I don't like the bus either. No, the field I'm talking about is not too far from where you live, Cam," said Sonja.

"Wait, how do you know where I live?" said Cameron, all frazzled.

"You have your address on your lunch bag, ya nerd," Sonja pointed out. "The field is just north of Eddy Street through a strip of woods. It's an old field."

"I remember playing catch with my dad there, but it wasn't the dad I know now. Do you ever get those memories that just don't make sense, like they might be from dreams or something? It's strange, but I know he was my dad. Anyway, I'm sure that my first baseball glove was a gift from him. I couldn't have been more than four or five, but there was something special about that time and that glove, playing catch with him." Cameron was suddenly startled and added, "I don't know why I'm telling you this; I don't even know you."

When he went back to where Bill and Kevin were sitting, they wanted to know all about the conversation he had just had with Sonja. Cameron brushed them off and acted like they hadn't asked anything and said, "Have either of you ever played on the old ball field near my house?"

"Sure, when we were younger and Memorial Field was being used. We haven't played ball for a long time, though, at least at a ball field," said Kevin, picking up the trash from his lunch.

"Yah, why would we want to play with amateurs when we have all of baseball's greatest players on the console?" said Bill.

"The difference is reality and getting some fresh air and exercise with real people," said Cameron rather judgmentally.

"You're one to talk, Cameron. You're whiter than all of us put together. King of the Cave Dwellers, that's you," joked Kevin.

Cameron would usually have joked back, but somehow, after his very first meeting with Sonja, he just didn't have the frivolity that he used to have. He didn't like this new seriousness that he saw in himself.

A random thought formed in Cameron's mind. It had a completeness about it that was unusual for him. His thoughts were normally not like this. "Sometimes change comes along and breaks you out of your comfort zone and regular routine. It forces you to look beyond yourself. Problems that you notice with this new view become personal and internalized. You could offer solutions, but would you? And why should you if you could?"

On Wednesday the following week, as Cameron was helping his mother bring in the groceries and putting them away, his mom suddenly asked him:

"I bumped into your home room teacher in the store and got talking with her. She tells me that you seem more distracted in class than usual lately. Does it have anything to do with the new student that just started?"

Cameron flushed red. "No, definitely not. It's probably because baseball season is about to start up and I can't wait to play. I'm thinking about trying out for the team this year," he said.

"That's a switch. You mean actually play outside on a baseball diamond instead of in front of your video screen?"
asked his mom.

"That's not fair. I can play real baseball," Cameron defended himself.

"I know that you can, but I'm just surprised that you would," said Mom.

"Well, Mom, to be honest, I did meet the new student. Her name is Sonja, and I can't believe it, but she loves baseball," confessed Cameron.

He was a little at a loss as to why he told her that and he was also a little giddy and lightheaded when he thought about Sonja. His confession to his mom made it hard for him to concentrate on his chores, and he didn't quite get to everything he was supposed to do.

Later that evening when Cameron finally started playing video games, he opted for his favorite baseball game. He could play it alone or with his friends, Bill and Kevin. He had other friends online that he would team up with on occasion, but this time he just wanted to play alone.

As he journeyed into the night, he suddenly became aware of the late hour and thought about whether he had washed the dishes or not. He went to the kitchen to check, and, sure enough, they were done and put away. Then he wondered if he had done them or someone else. Surely, they would have given him grief if that had been the case.

He headed back to his room and realized that it was not straightened up, nor the bathroom either. Everyone had gone to bed, and he thought that if he tried to clean up this late, he would wake them, so he didn't.

On his way back from the bathroom, he noticed a smell. Dog poop, unmistakable. As he passed the kitchen, he saw it by the back door.

Things were really getting out of hand. The dog had pooped on the floor below where the leash hung. Cameron thought how it must have been for the dog to agonize over needing to get out and finally relieving himself there at the door out of neglect. It made him feel really bad. So bad that he wanted to take Sandy out for a walk that very instant.

Cameron had been playing baseball on his video game console until the small hours of the morning—it was 3:30 a.m. now.

"Come on, Sandy, let's go for a walk," Cameron called softly.

Sandy was tired but reluctantly got up to have his leash attached, and out the back door they went. They headed towards the baseball field.

Cameron was nervous about going to the old ball diamond to play catch with Sonja. The stands were dilapidated, the water fountain didn't work because the local bullies would put sand in it all the time, and the fences were rusty and falling down. He gave Sandy a dog treat, but he only ate half of it and left the other half on the ground. Just before he took it from him, there was a flash of light, like lightning only without any thunder, and he couldn't tell where it came from. It made the hairs on his arms and the back of his neck stand up.

Here he was, at four in the morning, with Sandy standing where the gate would have been before the fence fell away. Suddenly there appeared a ribbon of light like a seven-foot-tall zipper that opened from top to bottom. Before he realized that he was not holding the leash tightly, Sandy bolted through the opening and was gone. The light split further open, and he frantically called for Sandy to come back. It felt like hours passed, but it was only about ten minutes. The strip of light began to close up, and with just enough space left, Sandy jumped back through, and it closed up the rest of the way and was gone.

"There's a good dog. Are you okay, Sandy boy, huh, where'd you go boy, huh?" he said as he rubbed his neck and hugged him. Cameron put his hands in his jacket because it was a bit chilly. The dog made a beeline for the biscuit that Cameron had given him before the light appeared. To his amazement the biscuit was whole. How could that be when he saw Sandy eat half of it? He distinctly remembered that the other half fell to the ground, and he had only brought one with him.

"You must be hungry now. You didn't much want it before … What am I saying?" said Cameron.

As he stood there puzzling over it, the entire event became ridiculous in his mind. He felt like his whole life was so out of whack in the first place, which explained why he'd thought it was right to take Sandy for a walk at four in the morning. Had the whole incident been his imagination?

As he crouched down and continued to pet Sandy and rub his neck, he started talking to him.

"How does it make sense to walk you at such an hour? I know that I'm just trying to catch up on my chores, but I should know that you have a routine for needing to be walked and going to the bathroom. You are a living being after all," Cameron reasoned.

"So are you, Cameron," came a familiar voice from the woods.

He froze. He thought that it sounded like Sonja, but that couldn't be. Why would she be way out here at this hour? But also, why was he here? Maybe his ears were playing tricks on him. After all, he had been rather preoccupied, thinking about Sonja and all the other things that seemed to be spiraling out of control in his life.

He decided to ignore it and take Sandy home. Just before he went to bed, he sent a text to the guys, asking to meet in the morning. He would only get a couple hours of sleep before he had to get up for school.

Cameron got up early before anyone else in the house and took his bike to meet the guys. Whenever there was something important to discuss, they would all meet in the parking lot of George's Astronaut Pizza House before school.

"I'm telling you it was like a seven-foot-tall zipper of light that opened up from the top down to the ground and Sandy jumped through it and was gone for about ten minutes," said Cameron.

"I've read about this kind of thing," said Bill.

"You mean in comic books, right?" said Kevin.

"No, for real."

"Well, when Sandy came back through, he went right for the biscuit that I had given him, and it was whole again, not just the half from him eating part of it," explained Cameron. "That means there is some kind of a time change thing going on. I'm hoping that it is all just my imagination, but ... I also thought that I heard Sonja's voice from the woods."

"Wait, I've seen that on Supernatural. The gateway to the alternate earth where everything is charred and burnt and demons are fighting a war with humans," said Bill.

"You know, that's not really helpful. You need to stop doing that," said Kevin. "Apparently something really did happen, and Cameron is pretty shaken up over it."

"Well, what are we going to do about it?" asked Bill.

"Well, tomorrow night I'm supposed to meet Sonja at the old field to throw the ball around. I'll go and do that, and then I'll go from there. I am not expecting anything to happen, but if it does, I'll let you know," said Cameron.

The next day there was not much interaction with Sonja, and it was a good thing since Cameron had to work on homework that he didn't get finished the night before. At lunch, however, she did remind him to meet at seven and added that he didn't have to bring his ball and glove.

"So, we're going to play catch and she's bringing the equipment, some kind of tomboy, right?" said Cameron to his friends as they were getting on their bikes to go home. "Don't get too far in the game without me. I'll have to get caught up with that too."

"Have fun on your date, Cam. Don't leave out any details when you tell us about it, lover boy," teased Bill.

When he got home, Cameron didn't want to tell his family where he was going for fear of being teased. They wouldn't leave him alone; they would all poke fun at him. It was 6:30 p.m. and they were supposed to meet at the field, so Cameron was in a rush to get finished so he could leave. After eating supper and doing up the dishes, there came a knock at the back door. Cameron felt shocks through his body. Why was he sure that it was Sonja at the door? He became anxious at the thought of Sonja being at his house instead of at the ballfield. He would have to change his story of going to the library to study.

It was hard for him to think on his feet in such a situation because he never had to before. His brother, Chuck, opened the door and invited her in. Right away Sonja introduced herself and told him that she was going to the library to study with Cameron. How did she know? He hadn't told her the story he had thought up to tell his family, and how did she know that he would have needed to make up a story to cover for what he considered to be a date?

"You didn't tell us that you were going to study with a friend," said his mom. "Where are you from, Sonja?"

"I'm from Boston. Our family is originally from Italy, though," she answered. "My folks thought we needed a less cluttered skyline."

“Well, we should be going now, Sonja. See you all later. Should be home around 8:30, 9:00ish,” said Cameron quickly, and ushered her out the door. “Why did you come to my house?” he asked when they were outside. “I thought we were supposed to meet at the field.”

“So, you’re ashamed of me, eh?” Sonja said as they started walking to the field.

They had to head off toward the downtown library and walk around the block so that nobody would be suspicious. Cameron thought, ‘Is this what young love makes you do?’

“I’m not ashamed; I just don’t want to be made fun of and teased. So, that didn’t work out too well, did it?” said Cameron. “So, your family is from Italy. Were you born there?”

“No, my grandparents came over with my parents just after they got married,” said Sonja. “It’s kind of too late to play a full game of baseball now, but if you want, we could just throw the ball around, get used to the place a little. We can come back another time with Bill and Kevin and some others and play a real game.”

They walked towards the ballfield, Cameron growing more nervous. He remembered the events from the night before. As if on cue, they approached the spot where the old ball field gate would have been, the zipper of light began to appear. Cameron froze again, turning to Sonja. He was surprised to notice that she didn’t seem to be shocked by it; rather, she acted as if she expected it to happen.

“Don’t you see that strip of light there!” Cameron cried, pointing to it as she looked him right in the eyes.

“Have you seen it before?” Sonja asked.

“I saw it last night, I, I saw my dog jump through it.” Cameron was panicked. “What is it? I thought that I was seeing things.”

“It’s nothing to be afraid of; it can’t hurt you,” said Sonja. “Did it hurt your dog?”

“Well, it didn’t hurt Sandy, but it did something weird,” said Cameron. “If I didn’t know better, I’d say that there was a time shift. I know that sounds pretty science fiction to you, but it’s the only way that I can explain it.” He took a deep breath to calm himself. “How is this happening?” Then he turned to face her straight on. “Do you … do you have something to do with this? Was it … was it really you that I heard that night?”

“Really, Cam, you don’t have anything to worry about. The only thing that will be shifting is your perspective on life. And trust me, that is for the better,” said Sonja.

“You are avoiding the questions! I need answers, or I’ll sound like I’m crazy to anyone I tell this to. Not that I have a lot of friends and just my family to tell, but that’s not the point. Do you get that?” asked Cameron. “I feel like I’m caught up in a dream every time I’m with you.”

“Now, that is nice to hear you say. I don’t know how far our relationship can go, but for now, I am pleased with it," said Sonja. "I will give you more information along the way, but this journey is only just beginning, Cameron. Don't you want to see where it goes? Sometimes change happens that breaks you out of your routine and comfort zone in life and forces you to see beyond yourself."

She beckoned to him, and he was obliged to follow. He felt oddly calm now. As they stepped through the ribbon of light, there was a sudden flash that intensified to a bright white burst. It slowly condensed and spread out to reveal a brilliant blue sky with puffy white clouds and a pristine, well-manicured baseball field at noon. It all had sort of a cartoon quality to it.

"What the hell?" Cameron yelled as he looked down at his hands and arms. "I look like CG! How is this happening?" He turned to Sonja who was standing next to him, totally calm. "You owe me an explanation!" he cried. "I'm having a hard time believing this is real."

"Let's play catch while we have the field to ourselves, Cam," said Sonja. "Just like in one of your video games. Just try to enjoy it for now. We'll get around to explanations in due time."

She had a full baseball uniform on and when Cameron looked at himself more closely, he discovered that he did too. Sonja went to home plate; Cameron took the pitcher's mound. He had no idea what was going on but decided to just go with it. There was a glove for each of them, and on the mound, there was a ball. Cameron reached down and grabbed the glove and ball; he was amazed to be able to actually feel them. He put the glove on, and it fit perfectly as he slammed the ball into it several times. Then he reared back and wound up to pitch and as he released it, had the sensation of releasing the buttons of his game console at just the right moment—only he wasn't playing a video game. As the ball soared toward home plate, it was followed by a vortex of a speed graphic, just like in a game. If Cameron hadn't been so freaked out by the experience, he would have been having fun.

Sonja caught the fast ball, letting out a puff of dust from her glove and a loud smacking sound, louder than it would have been in reality.

"This is too weird for me, Sonja. Are you going to explain what is happening?" Cameron asked.

"Just settle down and try to catch this high fly," Sonja said as the ball came screaming down out of the sky to him. Cameron caught it just in time but as if it were meant to be caught. It was like being in the catch zone of a video game hand when an object is either caught or dropped—it has to obey the coding built into the game.

"This is so strange," said Cameron, shaking his head. "Here, throw it back," he added as he hurled it to her.

"Here it comes, rookie," she said. Cameron held his glove out just short of where the catch zone would be, and the ball landed on the ground. He wanted to see if the direction of the ball would have been affected without his interaction with it. He was satisfied, knowing that it was not a 'can't lose' situation;

there was some skill involved. The whole thing looked and felt fake.

“Cameron, if there was something that you could do to make life better, would you do it?” Sonja suddenly asked. Why was she asking this now, in this strange situation?

“You mean for me, my life?” asked Cameron. “If you mean life for everyone else, no. For what? I would prefer life to go on without my involvement in it. Let someone else fix it.”

“But if you see solutions for life’s problems, problems that you didn’t even know existed, wouldn’t you, shouldn’t you try to offer those solutions? How could you go back to your old way of life knowing that you could have offered a solution?” she said with a melodious tone. “Why would you go back?”

Cameron just stared blankly at her and kept on catching and throwing the ball. Her words brought him back to the thought he had the day before he met Sonja. ‘Sometimes change comes along and breaks you out of your comfort zone and regular routine. It forces you to look beyond yourself. Problems that you notice with this new view become personal and internalized. You could offer solutions, but would you? And why should you if you could?’

After a long time of playing ball in this strange reality, Cameron was ready to go back.

“How do we get out of here, wherever this place is?” asked Cameron.

"You just have to want to, and I was going to tell you …" Sonja began to say as she came running up to the pitcher's mound. She began to move in slow motion, and everything became bright white light.

The next thing Cameron remembered was hitting his head while being put in his bed.

Chapter Two:

A Walk in the Woods

"What was it that you were going to tell ..." Then Cameron's dreams fade to black.

When he finally got up, it was earlier than he thought, especially for him on a Saturday. He noticed that he was wearing the same clothes that he had on from the day before. His head hurt a little. He quickly changed and began rushing around doing chores that hadn't been gotten to during the week. As he walked Sandy, bits and pieces of yesterday began coming back to him. When he was almost back home, he noticed Sonja on her bike just turning onto Eddy Street. He quickly brought Sandy back into the house. He was ready to face her with some questions. He opened the door, about to go after Sonja, just as she was about to knock.

"I'm glad you came over," he said immediately. "I want to talk to you about last night, the old ballpark. What the hell happened? Ever since I met you, it's like my life has been turned inside out. Are you some kind of witch or wizard? What was that place and why did I forget about it until I woke up this morning? I don't remember coming home and going to bed."

"Have you ever been to the woods around Snow Pond?" Sonja asked calmly, not even acknowledging that he had said anything. "I think it would be a wonderful place to explore, don't you?"

"Did you hear what I said?" cried Cameron. "I had strange dreams last night, and I don't know which were real and which were of that odd place we went to."

"Oh, hi, Cam. Good to see you too," Sonja said with sarcasm in her voice. "If you can believe it, I am trying to help you. Not only that, I'm trying to help humanity, your whole race."

That took Cameron by surprise. Was she kidding or just being overly dramatic? She seemed like a completely different person than she had been last night. He thought, 'Why did she say, 'my race'?'

"What do you mean? You didn't even know me a few weeks ago. How can something so disturbing be helpful?" asked

Cameron. "Sometimes I feel like you have a hallucinogenic effect on me, like a drug."

"You do remember what we did last night now, don't you?" she said.

"I don't remember leaving the field or getting home. What happened to me?" Cameron asked.

"It was just you and I in there. One day you will have a lot of others to help you, and then you will see how dynamic it can be. You never see the real players in the games you play online, just their avatar, right? This will be different once it is ready and set," said Sonja.

"You're not making a whole lot of sense right now. What are you doing over here, anyway?" asked Cameron.

"I want you to come with me on a walk in the woods, Cam," Sonja said matter-of-factly.

"Well, that is just odd," said Cameron. "Why would I want to do that? And especially on a Saturday?"

"I thought we needed to spend more time together, you know, try and get to know each other better," she said. "I know that I want to know you better ... and your friends."

"Hey, what do they got to do with it?" Cameron said kind of defensively. "I can tell you whatever you want to know about them." He sighed, resigning himself to going along with her. "So, maybe we should go on this little walk in the woods."

Snow Pond was surrounded by the Town Forest. Aspen Grove Cemetery is at its southernmost end, and its boundaries lie north of Pleasant Street and west of Aspen Street. Further north is the Quabbin Reservoir which takes up the northern third of Ware County. The man that works the grounds at the cemetery is always referred to as the Caretaker of the Forest. No one knows his name, but that's who he has been for as long as Cameron or any of his friends could remember.

As they walked along, the undergrowth became increasingly denser and the air mustier and heavier with moisture. There were trees, plants and undergrowth intertwined, all growing in harmony. Flowers and weeds, mushrooms and evergreen berries growing around the bases of trees older than Cameron's grandparents and in rotted tree trunks and limbs. Such growth, everywhere a profusion of vegetation.

"Life is change. Allow yourself to grow with the changes around you," said Sonja. "We need to get moving through the overgrown forest of life's problems."

There were vine swings hanging out over the river and Snow Pond, as well as some old logging two-tracks they would follow for a short distance. It seemed like Sonja wanted to get off the beaten trail and explore.

"I don't think that I would like morel mushrooms," said Cameron.

"You don't even want to try them?" asked Sonja.

"No."

"Then leave them alone, they are for someone else. There is a reason and a purpose for them," Sonja said rather matter-of-factly. "Something in the venue matrix intended for another subject," she mumbled softly.

Cameron thought her response was rather odd—even more so than usual. What did she mean by it?

"There is a vibrant life out here beyond the routine and safe life you now lead. Beyond just what you know. Walk in the world and discover the adventure in life, Cam," said Sonja.

They came to the cliffs along the eastern shore of Snow Pond, and they began to cautiously move along a narrow walkway ledge leading to a cave overlooking the large body of water. They inched their way along the strip of rock jutting out until they reached it. They entered the cave and discovered that it extended much further back than it first appeared. The further they went, the larger it grew until they came to a spot where the familiar ribbon of light began to open.

This set the hairs on the back of Cameron's neck to attention and with a shock of realization he knew that this might become a common mode of travel with Sonja. Hesitatingly, he entered it with her, and the cave became much larger on the other side and with signs of someone living in it.

"It looks like someone is living in here," said Cameron. "Could there be cavemen in this virtual reality world? I have some games like The Cave or Caveman, RPG games where you have to hunt animals to use for food and clothing. You have a shelter, a cave for your home and everything you do in the game is for your survival. When you kill your prey, you get trophies for the walls of your cave. The longer you can stay alive and the more trophies you receive, the more points you get."

"The people that live in the cave have to get their food and clothing from the animals they kill," said Sonja. "People working in the real-world scratch and claw at their jobs to be able to eat and to feed and clothe their children. The real problem is that they want to live a better life than everyone else. They strive for what they want, instead of what they need."

As Cameron looked down at what he was wearing, he noticed thick, coarse hair covering his arms and legs. Then he looked at Sonja. She had a unibrow and a square, chiseled jaw, but she was still there under the avatar. They both wore crudely made clothes of animal skins, but they fit right in the places they needed to most.

"Yes, Cameron, we've become those hunters of animals for food and clothing," said Sonja. "Isn't that an exciting scenario for us to play out? It might not be as fun as your video game version, though."

The cave opened up on the other side to a vast savanna with majestic mountains in the distance. They became the cave people that would have to chase down the prey and kill it with spears and clubs for food and hides to make their clothing.

As they began to run across the field, three more people came alongside them and motioned toward one of a small herd of some kind of tiny deer. The deer had disproportionately small legs and couldn't run very fast, so it was easy to chase them down. The people were not so much what Cameron would call cavemen. They were more like an alien race with primitive weapons. They were short and hairy all over, and all of them had on animal skins of some kind.

Two of the newcomers got a deer from one of the herds. Sonja got one on her own, and Cameron, with the help of the third character, knocked one down as well. The process was not as graphic as in real life, more like it would be a video game: the motion of bending down over the catch and moving your hands and arms suddenly produced meat, pieces of hide and tools made from the antlers and large claws from the hind feet. As they gathered the items up to put in shoulder bags that suddenly appeared, one of the other extra characters and then Sonja had a wardrobe change in a flash. Then, there appeared a statistics box over their heads, just like one would when a video game character got an upgrade in armor or weapons.

Cameron's weapon changed as well.

"This is too cool, just like being in a game!" said Cameron.

"Yah, the only bad part about it is that we don't have the real mess of the kill and field dressing the animals that are needed for food and the long process of tanning the hides, fitting, cutting and sewing the garments into clothing. That's what I want you to understand, Cam. It isn't as clean-cut, lay your money down, cash and carry like what you would buy in the grocery store for food. Life is much gritter than that," Sonja explained. "Man has come a long way in making survival clean and easy, but you need to see the hard work that went into making the process of what you call 'modern'. The art of survival has a long heritage, and many cultures have worked together to bring the manufacturing of food and clothing to its modern-day status."

"I believe that I appreciate it for what it is and where it came from. I just don't think about it all that much, or hardly ever, as a matter of fact," said Cameron. "What is it with these speeches and lessons? Are you some kind of premature professor sent to educate me on my days off school? Come on, I thought this was supposed to be fun."

"I think we are done with this scenario. We should head back," Sonja said abruptly. "I think that you think that you know more than you do. Maybe you do, but I believe that the understanding of your knowledge is flawed."

It seemed rather blunt for Sonja to reduce the game down to a pop quiz and then tell Cameron that he had failed. After all, she was the one that wanted to go for a walk.

"Why can't we just exit here?" Cameron asked.

"We need to bring the items back to the cave. You will see why when we do," she said.

As they headed back, Cameron asked, "By the way, what was it that you were going to tell me at the end of our game of catch at the old ball field last night?"

"Oh yes, it is a lot easier to leave a venue if you close your eyes and hold your breath for a few seconds. There isn't any blackout effect afterwards, and I don't have to help you to get home and to bed," she explained. "And you will remember the whole thing."

"Yes, I can see how that would have been good information to have. What did you have to do, carry me?" he asked, rather embarrassed.

"No, I just helped you walk. You become rather like a drunk that staggers and can't quite see where he's going," explained Sonja. "That being said, you also have to remember where you were between ten and thirty minutes before you entered the venue. That is where you will come out. So, if you recall, in this venue we were on the narrow walkway ledge above Snow Pond. Hopefully we won't lose our footing and fall into the water when we are ready to leave."

When they entered the cave and moved to where the skin-covered sleeping enclosures and fire was, the bag downloaded the items into an inventory. The listing appeared in the air just like a dialogue box in a video game. There came up a score that, to Cameron's way of playing, was pitiful: 12.5%.

"That's pretty bad. Can we go out again?" asked Cameron.

"No, we are done with this venue. You will have to make it up in other scenarios along the way," said Sonja. "Now, are you ready to leave?"

"Well, I don't really want to, but if that is really it, maybe we should," Cameron reluctantly conceded.

Cameron turned to face Sonja and when he did, he saw her wave her arm and, in the background, there were images of the cave but with other things going on in it. There was one like a prison with a lot of people dressed to look like they were from ancient Rome. Another had the cave set up like a banquet hall filled with people dressed in formal clothes. The chandeliers were made from deer antlers. With the wave of her arm, these and several other venues played through and were gone.

"What were those images, Sonja?" Cameron said with a gasp.

Sonja looked him in the eyes and said, "Other parts of the venue that you could have chosen to experience in this adventure, but it's enough for the first time. They could have brought you up to 20% if you did well with them. But 20% was the limit, and we can gain the 8% someplace else."

"This is going to sound crazy, but why can't I choose now?" Cameron let out a frustrated sigh. "Even as I ask that, it makes me feel like a little kid that has had a new toy taken away from him. What have you done to me and why?" said Cameron with confused anger.

For once, Sonja answered him point-blank and bluntly. "I have begun to open up your mind to see new horizons for the purpose of training you to think beyond the problems in the world to solutions that will work. Cam, you can't even imagine what your future holds."

With that, Cameron closed his eyes and held his breath and, in an instant, felt himself falling until he hit the cold water of Snow Pond. It was a good thing that he knew how to leave a venue this time, since he would have drowned if it were not for his being fully aware.

They both swam to the shore and got out of the water. The first thing Cameron thought of was starting a fire to warm them and to begin drying their clothes, but he knew that he didn't have any matches or other means of starting a fire. It was a brisk day in mid-October, but the sun was shining brightly. Maybe they would be all right.

"Look at your watch, Cam," said Sonja. "We went into the venue at precisely 10:12 a.m. So, what time is it now?"

"9:53, nineteen minutes before we went in. That's amazing, and I remember everything like it really happened," said Cameron.

"What do you mean? It did really happen, you nerd," she said.

"Not if I choose not to believe it. And there is no proof of it down to the very time it took to experience it," said Cameron. "I admit that there was an experience that I have in my brain, but what is it worth? You're going to have to convince me of its value; that it's better than having fun playing a video game. There's just too much other stuff, an agenda that I don't understand, for me to place any more importance to it than that. Sorry."

With that put aside, they spent most of the time walking back to Cameron's house hardly talking about anything other than school. When they got to the corner of Pleasant and Parker Streets, they said their goodbyes, and Sonja went on home. Cameron went home too, and there were Kevin and Bill waiting for him.

"Where have you been, Cameron? We have been waiting here

for over an hour." said Bill. "And why are you all wet?"

"Yah, we thought that you wanted to hang out and go get some pizza or something. Are we still on for gaming tonight?" asked Kevin.

"Sure, but I don't remember that we were going to do anything today. Not that we can't, I just went for a walk in the woods with Sonja is all," said Cameron. "We were in the Town Woods, and we fell into Snow Pond from the cliffs."

"What were you doing up there?" asked Bill. "Strange thing to do on a date."

"It wasn't a date," Cameron protested. "I'll go in and get changed, and we can go for pizza if you want to. Come on in."

"You know, Cameron, you don't have to be so defensive in your relationship with Sonja. We couldn't be happier for you. She gets you out of the house, your cave, even. She is kind of a tomboy, but you certainly could do a whole lot worse," Bill said, then added, "Mind you, I never see her hanging around the other girls at school though, do you guys?"

"Now that you mention it, no," said Kevin.

"And I only see her in the two classes that I have with her and on the weekends. Guys, you have to get me involved with more things on the weekends. It's not that I want to avoid her, but it's been every week lately," said Cameron. "Let me get changed, and I'll be right out so we can go."

"We'll be here. Can't wait to hear the rest of the story," said Kevin.

Cameron didn't say much as they all got on their bikes to head to George's Astronaut Pizza House, and they couldn't talk much on the way. He was trying to decide if he wanted to say anything about the light gate incident this time, and when they arrived, he was committed to telling them the story without the virtual venue part; unless they specifically asked, based on their reaction to the story he told them about the old ballpark. Cameron was beginning to wonder how much he should involve his friends in something that he didn't fully understand until he got to a place where he could be confident that they would accept it. He didn't know whether he accepted it yet, but something about Sonja made him want to keep seeing her. Something strange, not like love, but a sense of wonder at what she was showing him about himself and his life. A longing for purpose, perhaps? He didn't know.

Cameron was having thoughts and impressions that were very adult in the sense that he was surprised about dwelling on issues that much more mature people would concern themselves about. Why was Sonja so intelligent and how could she turn it on and off so that when they were around others, she was just one of the guys and when they were on one of her adventures, she was like some old professor and Cameron was her only student? He knew that she didn't get out much when she lived in Boston, but Cameron wondered what her friends could have been like.

They ordered the extra-large, deluxe Saturn pizza and took their regular table in the corner. There was a lot of small talk as they waited for the food to come, and Cameron got a feel for what would satisfy their curiosity about his walk in the woods with Sonja.

"So, nature hike, you were collecting plant samples for a class assignment, right?" asked Bill with a little sarcasm. "Were they underwater plants?"

"No, Sonja just wanted to get away from town. She hardly ever had a chance when she lived in Boston. I know the area, and she invited me to be a kind of guide," Cameron said. "The fall into Snow Pond was an accident. You know, if one of you would like, I could offer your services to her the next time she wants to go for a walk."

"We wouldn't think of invading your territory, Cam. At this point, we are content to just hear about your exploits and adventures," said Kevin. "But tell us, why were you up on the cliffs?"

"She knew about a cave that she wanted to explore. It was directly over the water. The walk ledge was slippery, and we fell," said Cameron. He was out with it before he realized that she couldn't possibly know about a cave in the cliffs, being from out of town. "I guess she heard about it from another friend from school," he added.

"Then, why would she want you to go with her and not this

other friend?" said Bill. "I think that there's more than just friendship happening here."

Cameron felt that he had salvaged his tale with his quick thinking. Suddenly, Kevin announced, "Here comes the pie, and look over there at who's sitting with I don't know who?"

They all looked and saw Sonja across the room with some other boy about their same age, eating and talking.

"Do you know him, Cam?" asked Bill. "He looks about our age, but I don't remember seeing him at our school."

"No, I can't say that I've ever seen him either," said Cameron, shaking his head. "But it doesn't bother me. The thing that I can't understand is how she got here so fast after obviously going home to change first. That's not what she was wearing earlier, and she lives over in the Maple Street Annex."

"Well, she is a mystery, and we don't believe that it doesn't bother you a little," said Kevin. "So, do you want to find out who he is? I'll go over there and find out for you."

"No, we're fine here. Let's just eat our pizza, and maybe she won't notice us," said Cameron. "Are you guys ready for the game tonight?" he asked, trying to change the subject. "Who will carry through the dungeon?"

"You can deflect and distract all you want, Cam, but we know that you have a thing going with Sonja. I'll carry through the dungeon tonight since I have the highest level so far," said Bill.

"You two can grab all the loot you can find, and we should be about even when we come out."

They got down to the real business of discussing the game and eating pizza. When they were ready to leave, Kevin and Bill went on ahead, but Cameron was stopped by Sonja as he walked past her table. The boy that she was sitting with had already left.

"How in the world did you get here so fast?" asked Cameron in hushed tones. "You had to go home to change first, didn't you?"

"Oh, hi, Cam. Have you been here long? No, I called my mom and she picked me up with a change of clothes. Then she dropped me here to meet with Peter to set up a time when we could go for a walk in the woods," Sonja said. "Do you remember, the morel mushrooms were for him."

"Yah, we were across the way at our usual table having pizza, Bill, Kevin and me. We didn't notice that you were here," Cameron lied. He realized that she had to be there long before he and his friends arrived. Suddenly, he had a thought about the boy she was with. "Will you go to the cave with him too?" he asked. "This Peter. Shouldn't I know him? Isn't he from our school?"

"No, Cameron, he's from Woodland Academy, a private school, and I have a lot of potential recruits to train," said Sonja with a commanding tone.

Cameron was shocked by her sudden change in demeanor. She had never addressed him by his full name before, and the interchange he just had with her was rather disorienting for him. He thought that he would play along rather than force her to explain it. He imagined it as a glitch and added it to his list of things that were strange about Sonja.

Cameron was at a place where he really wanted to confide in someone about this whole situation, but who could it be?

"They just left, and I have to get home to do chores.
We have a game time set up for tonight. I'll see you in school on Monday, K?"

Cameron wasn't sure what he had gotten himself into but there was enough intrigue to make him want to see it through and to have his questions answered. He couldn't get it out of his head all the way home on his bike. He kept thinking that it sure would be nice to have someone to confide in. More and more he felt that he needed someone to bounce it off of or he might just think that he was going a little crazy.

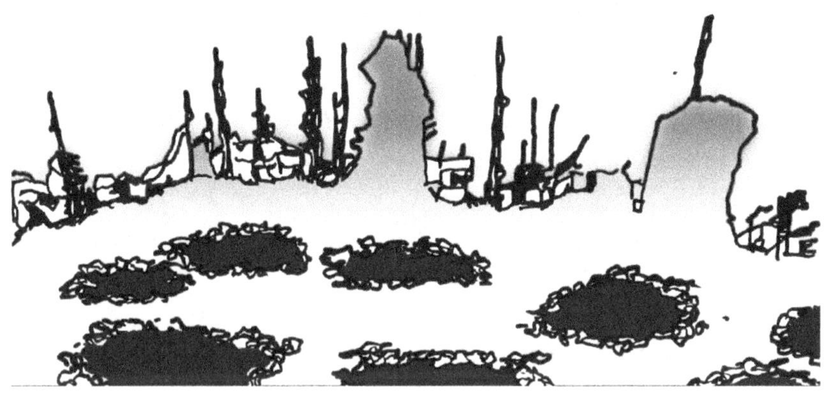

Chapter Three:

The Zoo

When Cameron woke up the next morning, he just lay there in bed, staring at the ceiling and thinking about the day before. There was so much for him to take in and process that he almost forgot that he didn't have to get up and go to school. He thought about the place through the light gate; how that if he knew that it played like a video game, he could have done much better and gone through all of the scenarios and racked up a lot of points. But then he began to wonder, what were the points good for and why did Sonja pick him to be involved in this crazy thing?

He got up and started his day with all these things in the back of his mind. It was Saturday, mid-morning. Suddenly, there was a knock at the front door. Cameron's dad had left to play golf and his mom was doing the laundry. He didn't know where his brother had gone, but that was usually the case with Chuck. He went to answer the door, and to his surprise, it was Sonja. She was sitting on the front steps and jumped up when Cameron opened the door.

"I think that we should go to the zoo today. What do you think, wouldn't that be fun?" asked Sonja.

"Well, I never liked the idea of animals held in cages, but I do like animals," said Cameron. "Why don't you want to get some of the guys together and play some baseball?

"Come on, Cam, you know you don't have enough friends to play a decent game," said Sonja. "We can go to the old field later and play a real game."

"And just how are we supposed to do that if we don't have enough players?" asked Cameron.

"You leave that up to me and you'll see," she explained. "I want you to get out more and enjoy your surroundings. You have a lot of opportunities with your life, Cam; no sense not seeing what your interests are."

"Why are you so interested in my future? What are you doing this for, a class project?" asked Cameron rather puzzled. "It's like you are two separate people. Before we go off to do some crazy adventure, you're one person, and when we enter the venues, you become someone else. I have to be honest with you, Sonja, I'm a little afraid of you."

"Well, for one thing, I never had many occasions where I was able to get out and explore the world in Boston. You would think that there would be a lot to do and see, but both of my parents worked all the time, and I was usually left home in an apartment with my little sister. I only got to see the world whenever we went on vacation, which wasn't very often," she explained. "I feel so alive and free here, though. Don't you feel caged up, sitting at your computer all the time?"

Cameron stepped back into the house and yelled to his mom.

"Mom, I'm going to the zoo with Sonja. We should be back for supper. Is that alright?" he asked.

"Fine, I guess. Really, the zoo?" his mom answered from the laundry room with confusion in her voice.

"Don't worry, Mrs. Adams, I'll vouch for his sanity," chimed in Sonja from the porch.

Cameron was beginning to think that Sonja was more mature and experienced in dealing with adults and social situations than she let on.

The trip to Ludlow where the Lupa Zoo was located took just under an hour by train. Along the way, they began to talk.

"It seems strange to me that we put animals in cages to protect and preserve them because they are endangered in the wild, but we want to rescue them and perpetuate them so we can put them back in their environment," said Sonja, ignoring Cameron's comments. "It seems like a vicious, never-ending cycle to me. What do you think, Cam?"

"We place the animals in cages for the world to see in case the whole species were to become extinct. We mean it for conservation, for their survival," said Cameron, going along with the change of subject. "We care for them in a world that has become too unbalanced for their safety. We want to rescue them."

"Just as we need to be rescued, Cam. Can you see yourself sitting at your computer in a cage in this zoo?" joked Sonja. "Mankind is endangered and doomed to extinction unless the fittest are trained to solve the problems of true unbalance in the world. Good over evil, love of others over love of self. Can you see yourself coming up with those kinds of solutions?"

"There you go again. What is it with putting the problems of the whole world on my shoulders?" asked Cameron. "I think that I have good balance with my life the way it is."

He had to admit to himself that what he just said wasn't completely true, but Sonja couldn't know that. Or could she?

Getting off at the station, they were met by a group of people that included several of their classmates who were just hanging out in the quaint, downtown district of the town.

"I had no idea that kids from our town came here to hang out," said Cameron. "You're right, I should get out more."

As they strolled along the downtown streets of Ludlow, they came to a trolley stop with one just pulling up to it. The Lupa Zoo was one of the destinations on the trolley light sign, so they got on.

"You have to promise me that you won't want to bring any of the animals home with you when we leave," said Sonja. "No matter how adorable they are."

"All I can imagine is that they will look like all the dogs and cats that you see on the television ads for adoption. Sad, watery eyes, shivering. Why would I want that? I have Sandy," said Cameron. "He's a happy dog."

They pulled up to the stop in front of the entrance gate to the zoo and got out. The admission fee wasn't too bad, and as soon as they went in, Cameron saw a hot dog stand. It reminded him that he was really hungry, and he bought two of them with all the fixings. Then he asked Sonja if she wanted one. When she said yes that she did, he ordered another one for her. He started munching on them as they proceeded to the exhibits. They didn't get too far before he had finished both of them.

After visiting the Asiatic black bear, the camel, the yak, the binturong and the giraffe, they went through the small creatures like spiders, lizards, hedgehogs and lemurs. Sitting down for a time on one of the benches surrounded by painted animal statues, they rested for a while.

“We should sit here for about twenty-five or thirty minutes before we go in,” said Sonja. “It will be a pleasant place to come back to.”

Cameron sat uncomfortably, not knowing what to say. He was thinking about the strange interaction they had had at George’s Astronaut Pizza House. He thought it would be good to start with asking. That usually worked.

“So, Sonja, is there anything you would like to let me in on about what you are doing as a trainer?” said Cameron casually. “What is that all about? I mean, you have this Peter guy that goes to Woodland Academy. How did you even meet up with him? Is it a job you have working as a tutor or something?”

“You could say that I am working for an organization to train gifted individuals,” said Sonja. “I don’t think you should worry or be concerned. It’s nothing that can hurt our relationship.”

“What relationship? I am not sure what our relationship even is, teacher. How am I ‘Gifted’?” asked Cameron.

“You’ll see, I think that you are already beginning to see. It takes a little time. Which reminds me, we should get going,” she said.

They both stood up, and somehow the light gate was beginning to form in front of them. One step and they were both through to the venue.

Cameron found himself on a high hillside overlooking a massive city that had been decimated, smoldering in heaps of rubble. There had been a great battle, and by the looks of it, the weapons of the enemy were indefensible. It looked as though all were lost. As he focused in more, he noticed in among the ruins, large circles of built-up rubble with clearings in the middles. There was some sort of ship that had landed there, and as he looked out over the distant horizon, there were hundreds of these rings. He wondered what they could be and what was going on.

The ships in the center of the clearings had a line of box-like frames spiraling around them which appeared to be moving slowly toward the inside of the ships. Cameron was not able to make out exactly what was happening, so he began making his way down the hillside to walk along one of the devastated city streets. There was silence, and the skies were filled with dark clouds. He knew that it was not nighttime; the sun just refused to shine through, as if creation were turning its face away from so much destruction.

"Is this the state of the entire planet in this scenario, Sonja?" asked Cameron.

“Everything has been wiped away. All that defined them as human. Every accomplishment and original idea, every achievement and advancement in all disciplines. How can they ever bounce back from this, Cam?” Sonja asked.

When he reached the rim of the closest ring, he started to climb to the crest. It was about twenty-five or thirty feet high, and as he reached the top; he saw the scene was far from pleasant. There were enclosures all along the inside wall of the circle that spiraled into the ship; and there were people inside them. They were in cages. In the middle sat the large ship. It was like nothing he had ever seen before, even in the video games that he played. It was of alien origin, of course, and the alien beings were loading the cages into the ship.

The beings themselves were huge, standing about ten feet tall and dressed in what looked like some type of military uniforms, but he would hold judgment until he knew more. He thought it to be military, given the context.

“What do you think they are doing, Cam?” asked Sonja.

“It looks like they are abducting the humans, taking them to their planet,” said Cameron.

“But the ship hasn’t left, what makes you think that they are being taken away?”

“I have seen the ships in the distance taking off and a new ship comes in right behind it to continue loading the people from the cages,” said Cameron, shaking his head in disbelief. “Tell me, Sonja, how is this anything like what we do when we put animals in a zoo? We're not destroying their world and taking them away just to put them in some great big collection in order to look at them."

"Are you sure that is what they are doing?" asked Sonja. "I think that we need to investigate further, don't you? Things can look a certain way on the surface, but the more you know about the reason and purpose the better. There could be a logical answer for what we are seeing.

"Right now, what you have observed is that terrible things have happened to Earth, predicated by an alien race that you perceive wants to enslave humans."

"Well, they might be taking them for slaves or for food," said Cameron. "I have to admit; we just don't know yet."

"That is exactly right, and until we do, don't you think that we need to see if we can communicate with the ones in the cages or with the actual aliens themselves?" she asked.

They carefully made their way down the inside of the encircling rubble ring and came close to one of the cages. There were six people inside. Cameron gently approached and asked them what was going on.

"What? Don't you know anything? It's been over three years now since the Krawlar invasion. Why don't you know what's going on?" said one of the younger men in the cage.

“We are not from here. We want to understand what is going on, in order to help,” said Cameron. “Are you being taken against your will?”

“No, indeed not. We are being helped by the Vortak. They are the ones that are fighting the Krawlar; they’re trying to transform our world into a habitable environment again,” said one of the older men. “We are in line to be bio-enhanced in order to survive New Earth.”

As Cameron talked to more people in the cages, he thought that he had put the whole story together. Just over three years ago, the Krawlar race arrived in orbit with an ultimatum—if Earth would surrender and allow them to take over, reducing themselves to slaves, the Krawlar would not completely wipe out the human race when they destroyed the cities in order to make way for their own settlements. When Earth refused and chose to fight, the Krawlar poisoned the air. Three billion people were killed, and then the bombing raids began. Every major city on Earth was hit, killing an additional two billion.

The Vortak arrived and released a cure for the poison and a procedure to biologically enhance humans to give them immunity to the toxins that were introduced into the environment by the Krawlar. The effects of the toxins harmed the people, as well as the animals of earth. There were reports of some of the people and animals being taken by the Krawlar to be placed in their zoos, as well. That was not their main goal, though. They were looking for a world to conquer, occupy and enslave for their own use.

From what Cameron could gather, the Vortak followed the Krawlar throughout the galaxy, attempting to put right what the Krawlar decimated. They would exterminate the Krawlar as their weapons and technology were far superior, and restore the worlds attacked by them to health. They had the ability but not the will to wipe out the whole Krawlar race altogether.

"So, Cam, this is what you see here. Two alien factions at war on Earth. The planet is being destroyed, and one alien race is trying to harvest humans for slaves and to put in their zoos. The other race is trying to save them by wiping out the other race, curing the remaining humans and giving them bio-enhancements to be able to survive and rebuild their world. Is that right, did I leave anything out?" asked Sonja. "If this scenario were true, is this solution one that you would encourage, rebuild earth and populate it with bio enhanced versions of mankind?"

"That would be 180 degrees better than being enslaved to another hostile race or completely annihilated by them," said Cameron.

"But, Cam, wouldn't you welcome a race of beings that are so much further advanced than you, to be able to put things right, to engineer a new way to exist in a new world?"

"Somehow, that is not what is going on here. There should have been enough people loaded into that ship for it to have taken off and another one brought in to take its place. We need to find out what is really going on," said Cameron. "If they are taking them to some medical facility to get the bio-enhancement rather than doing it right on the ships, then why should it take so long to load them. I don't see anyone coming off the ship, so where are they taking them? We need to find that out."

Before Sonja could warn him, Cameron started off toward one of the Vortak beings who was standing along the line near the opening to the ship's cargo bay. They had not taken notice of him or Sonja all the time that they were questioning the people in the cages, but now the very tall Vortak man bent down to acknowledge him.

"Do you speak my language?" Cameron asked.

There came a garbled static burst and then the alien words that were coming from his mouth were broadcast to Cameron in English.

"No, but the translator implant that we have can translate your speech and ours. What do you wish to ask and why are you and your companion not in a crib?"

"We are not from here," said Cameron. "What are you doing with the people in these cages?"

After a short while the static burst back.

"We are loading them into the ship to take them to be prepared. I will provide you with a crib so that you can join the others," said the tall Vortak being.

He walked off toward a stockpile of empty cages to grab one and bring back. Cameron had a sudden urge to quickly duck into the ship—perhaps it was survival instinct kicking in. He moved to one side of the loaded cages and scurried along the hull wall. There were cages stacked to the ceiling of the cargo bay; there wasn't much more room to load any more. Mechanical arms grabbed the cages as they were conveyed into the door opening. They were lifted into the next available space and interlocked in place with special latches built into the cages. He thought that it was a strange way to transport them unless they wouldn't like what the end of the trip afforded them.

Cameron found a place to hide between the cages along the wall of the hull. He would wait and see where they were being taken to and try and get more information from the ones in the cages.

"How did you get out of your crib?" asked an older man in the cage Cameron was next to. "It may be a bumpy ride."

"I was never in one, but why do you call it a crib; I see it as a cage?" asked Cameron. "Crib is what the Vortak call them."

"Yes, and the idea of crib is what the Vortak got confused about due to our explanation of how medical procedures like surgeries were performed, with the patient lying down on a bed and being anesthetized. They didn't have a good definition for bed, so what they came up with was crib. We will all be put to sleep and bio-enhanced in order for us to be able to survive in the harshness of the environment of Earth as it is after the wars," the man explained. "We are being taken for processing."

Suddenly, Cameron had instant apprehensions about the intentions of the Vortak. He feared what would happen if his apprehensions were realized. As he remained hidden, he heard the gradually increasing roar of another approaching ship. Most likely coming to replace the one he was on, and to load more cages. He knew now that the loading of this ship was almost complete. The bay door began to close and when it did, there was complete darkness; not a good way to transport your guests that you wanted to take care of. The ship took off, and Cameron could feel the acceleration as the ship went rushing through the sky.

It didn't take long before they were landing again. The ship was on about a 45-degree angle as the bay door began to open and the cribs or cages began to be slid out all in one large, connected block. They were all connected, and Cameron noticed that they were all interlocked on every side, above and below forming a giant skid of cages.

They came to rest on a large, raised floor made of some type of metal. Many more skids were stacked along the edges of the floor, waiting to be transported away to be loaded with more people again. There was a strong smell that Cameron recognized from his experiences of hunting trips with his dad. When you field dress a deer and the warmth of the internal organs of the freshly killed animal meets the cold air of winter, it releases a smell that you never forget. This sent a quiver up

Cameron's spine, and the worst thoughts imaginable crossed his mind. His face showed real life, wide-eyed, jaw-dropped fear for all of the people that he knew were slaughtered and that were about to be slaughtered. The race that Cameron thought were here to save the human race were here to eat them.

Cameron held his breath and closed his eyes and instantly regenerated at the Lupa Zoo, twenty-six minutes and thirty seconds in the past. He fell to his knees and felt sick. The idea that it had not been real helped him a little to gather his wits about him just before he threw up the hot dogs with all the fixings that he had eaten earlier.

"I'm sorry for the realism of that scenario. Didn't mean for it to make you lose your lunch, Cam," said Sonja calmly. "I know that you will have a lot of questions about this one, right?"

There's the old Sonja back again, Cameron thought. "Sure do," he said, "like what does this sci-fi apocalypse have to do with a zoo, right off the top of my head?"

"Well, that's easy," Sonja said with a know-it-all attitude. "What did the walk in the woods have to do with a cave and hunting down your food for clothing and a tool cabinet? That was designed to teach you about discovery, adventure, change, growth, life." Then, with a softer tone, "The venue here at the zoo is to teach you what it means to be caged up; to teach you about conservation, rescue, what it means to be endangered, how we face extinction, how we care for one another, and why survival is important."

“And you think that I got all that?” asked Cameron. “It’s like being in a science fiction movie, only I wasn’t acting. The only reason that I didn’t leave sooner was because I knew that it wasn’t real, but you know that it is real, to a point.”

“Yes, Cam. It’s a story that you get the picture for. All of the information is there for your brain to work with and the addition of virtual reality, even down to the detail of smells and touch, it’s as if you lived the experience. We know that learning is made easier when all of your senses are engaged,” said Sonja. “Are you ready to go or do you need more time to acclimate to reality again?”

“We can go,” said Cameron. “And on the way you can tell me who this ‘we’ is that you mentioned just now. Also, I’m really hungry after losing my lunch. You wouldn’t think that I should be after that, would you?”

“What? That was just a slip. You most likely won’t want to eat any more hot dogs from the stand over by the entrance gate, right?” she said. “Let’s see what’s available in Ludlow. We’ll have plenty of time to find someplace and eat before the next train leaves. And don’t worry, you will be able to get back for your game night tonight, no problem.”

They did just that. They had fish and chips at Tony & Pennies restaurant. All the while Cameron had the thought in the back of his mind that the ‘we’ was not a slip-up, and it gave him an uneasy feeling that made him wary of getting to know Sonja better; on the other hand, he had to get to know her better to understand what was going on.

Chapter Four:

The Museum

"Once you have tasted flight, you will forever walk on the earth with your eyes turned skyward, for there you have been, and there you will always long to return." Leonardo da Vinci

"Meet me over by my place at 6:30," said Sonja. "We'll be going to the Ware Center Meeting House and Museum."

When Cameron rounded the last corner before arriving at the Pizza House, he saw that Bill and Kevin were already inside. A third bike was also there that he did not recognize. When he went in, he noticed the guys at their usual table with a large pizza already set in the middle of it. He glanced around the restaurant and didn't see anyone that could have ridden the other bike; it was mostly older people.

"Here's your cup. We weren't sure if you wanted root beer or Coke," said Kevin.

"Who owns the other bike out there?" Cameron asked as he sat down. "Someone new you invited?"

"Not us," said Bill.

With a scrunched-up, overexaggerated face, Kevin said, in a menacing tone, "It's Peter; he's here alone. At least we haven't seen Sonja yet. Warning, he went to the bathroom about five minutes ago. By the way, thank you for the assist in the game last night. It felt like you were back to your old self for a change."

"Thanks, I don't think that I did too well on the zoo outing, though. It was the most intense one so far, and I wasn't able to finish it. I never saw the end of the scenario; I couldn't take it anymore when I learned that people were food for the aliens," said Cameron shuddering. "There were two races of aliens, and the one that I thought was there to help the human race turned out to be the one that wanted to harvest people for food. It might have been that the first race, the Krawlar, were really the ones that were there to help, or maybe neither one was.

I might have found that out if I hadn't bailed. Regardless, my score couldn't have been too high… I forgot to ask Sonja what it was."

"What does that have to do with a zoo?" Bill asked. "Did you say that 20% was a perfect score for each venue? If that's the case, there should be only five that you have to ace, right? If there were more, it would probably be to make up the points for the ones that you do badly in."

"Twenty percent is the high point that you aim for, but you can earn more. All that I know is that all I have earned so far is 12.5%; but when you're in the scenario, you're not interested in making points, you're just caught up in the reality of it—or virtual reality of it, I should say. Sonja said that I would have to make it up in other scenarios along the way, make up the other 7.5 %. I don't know how much I earned from the zoo or if I will have to go through more scenarios or if I have to go through every single one she has, just to see just how high my score can go. I'm not sure how well I'm doing. If it's like a test every time I go with her, I feel like I'm failing," said Cameron. "I do feel like I'm getting to know Sonja more like a person though, someone that I can call … a girlfriend."

"As much as you want to believe that this relationship is real, man, look at the evidence. What about Peter and the fact that she never wants to include us in any of the adventures you tell us about? I think we need to see them for ourselves if you want us to really believe 'em. Why would she suddenly come here and pick up with you for these so-called 'lessons' she claims to be teaching you, and for what?" asked Kevin. "We have to stick together if we want to figure this out."

"Yes, Cameron, we think that it's too good to be true, and everyone we talk to at school does too; they can't understand it," said Bill. "Have her include us in one of these scenarios next time."

"I definitely will ask her, but I think that we are going to play baseball one of these days, and I think that she intends for you to join us. I have a lot of unanswered questions myself, but I can't say that it's been a waste of time. I'm definitely learning things through these virtual experiences that I just can't get in school, and I want to see it through," said Cameron. "She wants me to meet her at the Ware Center Meeting House and Museum tonight around 6:30. I think I'll show up early for this outing and hide out until she shows up. I want to see her mom or dad, if they drop her off."

As they prepared to leave George's Astronaut Pizza House to go home, Cameron didn't even fight over who would get the leftover slices. He planned to go home and walk Sandy and then take off for the museum in plenty of time to get there before Sonja. He hoped she would get a ride, but she might walk or ride her bike.

Across the street from the Ware Center Meeting House and Museum is a little fenced in area where Cameron sat waiting for Sonja to show up. It was an overcast evening, and he was sure that she would not see him as he crouched down behind the fence.

After a while, Cameron began to disregard the few cars that would roll by and focused on the sidewalks for bike traffic or walkers. Just then, two cars came by slowly, and after the second one, he thought that he saw someone standing on the sidewalk in front of the Center. As he took a closer look, Cameron thought that Sonja had come through a light gate, but he didn't see a ribbon open and close. Sonja just sort of shimmered into place, and as Cameron was regaining his composure from the shock of it, he got on his bike and went down the street and across while she was looking off in the other direction, to come up the street on the other side. He hardly made a sound so he could hear her talking to somebody, but there was no one there. He didn't see a phone either, so what could it be? He thought he heard her say, "I'll see you in the workshop; just be ready." Whatever that was supposed to mean.

Coming up from behind, Cameron made a loud arrival announcement as he suddenly blurted out, "Sorry that I'm so late, the guys were extra talkative *and* hungry today."

"Well, I haven't been here long," she said. "Are you ready to go in?"

Cameron looked toward the museum which was situated far in from the sidewalk. "Sure, how did you get here? I don't see your bike," he asked as he locked his bike to the stand in front of the museum.

"I was dropped off," Sonja lied. Cameron felt upset at her deception, but he held it in.

"I thought that we would go in and look around a bit before we jumped into a venue. Have you ever been inside here before?" Sonja asked. "A lot of local history here."

They walked up to one of the two doors. "I think we had a field trip once when I was in elementary school, but I don't remember much of it," said Cameron. "You kind of grow up hearing the stories and they just don't seem to be that important after a while. Kind of sad, isn't it? I mean, that's what they preserved all of it for, right?"

"Built in 1799, the meeting house was the center of life in Ware, a New England community. It served as a church and the first town hall. In 1986, the building was heavily damaged in a fire. Pictures show town residents and firefighters working to save artifacts from the building," said Sonja as if she was recollecting personal knowledge of the incident. "The non-profit Proprietors of the Ware Center Meeting House, Inc. was formed to oversee the restoration of the building. The Proprietors received a Massachusetts Historical Commission grant to repair the sanctuary walls and ceiling, and to restore and paint the outside of the building. Since then, the building has a new roof and museum quality restoration of the kitchen. They also built a shed to replicate a horse shed with recovered wood from the Ware-Gilbertville covered bridge."

"There you go with your Wikipedia presentation again. Where do you get this stuff from?" asked Cameron. "It sounds so rehearsed."

"I like to give the lessons a proper introduction, and actually, it is rehearsed, if you must know, thank you very much," she returned.

They went in and started looking around at the rooms which had been restored to the way they were in the early days. There were only a few people in the museum that afternoon. Cameron hadn't expected it to even be open on a Sunday.

Looking through the things that were of the latest technology for their day reminded Cameron of how far mankind had come and how good they had it in the present. From spinning wheels and pot bellied stoves to readymade cloths and solar panels for heat and electricity.

They went into the kitchen, and as they moved toward the right-hand corner, a ribbon of light began to form from top to bottom. Just as they were about to step through it, two young ladies with a small boy came into the room. Instantly, Sonja moved back, and the ribbon disappeared. The three looked over at them as if they had caught something out of the corner of their eyes. They had reacted in time though, and nothing was revealed, but now they would have to wait.

"It's good that we have to wait a little. The time shift difference is something that I always forget about. If we can wait twenty or thirty minutes, we will be put right back in this room when we return," Sonja whispered. "I always forget that part."

"Why are we doing this in such a public place, right out in the open for?" asked Cameron in a whisper back.

"I didn't think that there would be anybody else here on a Sunday," she said. "Especially at 6:30 in the evening."

They both stood still, just looking at each other for a while saying volumes with their eyes but neither one knowing what the other was saying.

"Have you ever played chess, Cam?" asked Sonja.

"Yes, but I'm not very good at it," he said.

"A lot of what your future may be is like a grand game of chess," said Sonja.

"How is that?" asked Cameron.

"Think of it this way. Products, made in America, high quality but expensive. Then along comes a cheap version of the same thing made somewhere overseas. It does about the same thing and undersells your American product to the point of the company having to go out of business, going broke. You know that the American made one was superior, but they just couldn't compete.

"Now what if you came up with something that just couldn't be beat?" said Sonja. "Quality, performance, price and a patent that couldn't be infringed upon? It could be something that is so far advanced, something that no one ever thought of before. It becomes one of your most powerful pieces in the life game of chess that you use to block or drive your opponent into whatever direction you wish them to go. Checkmate."

"Sorry, Sonja, but I don't have a clue what you are talking about," said Cameron. "But I do get the concept. Other countries always get around or away with bypassing our patent laws. Come on, out with it. What are you getting at?"

"I'm getting at the fact that if something is done for the benefit of humanity, there wouldn't be a problem with patent infringement. So, Cam, here is an example. Many places in the world need clean water for drinking and cooking. You come up with an instrument that can drill a well hole down past the water pocket into bedrock using graviton particle displacement—"

"Hold it right there," interjected Cameron. "What are you talking about? We are not in the scenario yet, are we? There is no such thing as graviton particle displacement. You're making it up."

"I'm talking about your future, Cam. You may come up with it," Sonja said looking down at her watch. "They have been gone for a little over thirty minutes; we can go in now."

"We can go in, but I'm not done with this conversation," Cameron said. "You're starting to sound a little crazy."

Sonja ignored him, approached the corner again, and the crackle and shimmer of the light ribbon began to open. Cameron sighed and followed her. When they stepped through, they were in a place where they had no indication of floor or ground, or up or down. The heavens were strewn out before them, and the vantage point was as if they were floating out among the stars in space. The images of the Hubble Space Telescope had nothing on what they were seeing.

"Sonja, I'm not too sure about this," said Cameron very nervously. "What's the plan? Even if I stay perfectly still, I feel like I am moving. Should we wait?"

"Yes, calm down. It will resolve itself into the scenario soon enough," said Sonja. "Just look at it. The incredible display of creation. This is what we are a part of, Cam. Doesn't that get your blood pumping?"

The scene started to draw toward a vanishing point in what became the middle of everything, and as the entire universe began to slowly accelerate past them, Cameron thought that he was going to be sick.

"Hang in there, Cam. We are going to be fine," said Sonja. "This is just setting the stage for our arrival."

"Where? Our arrival to where?" questioned Cameron.

Star fields, galaxies, nebulas and planetary systems started coming at them faster and faster. Moons and planets sped by until their own Solar system became recognizable, and the scale slowed down to within a tolerable speed.

There was a montage of images of things and people, inventions and famous figures from throughout time. Most of them Cameron didn't know by face until they were shown associated with what they were credited with inventing. He would know some of them, but they came at him so fast that he could hardly believe that they were going to be useful or practical information. Even if he were able to flip through the images at his own pace, how could this prepare him for what was coming?

Suddenly, they found themselves in a room. It was crudely round with seven doors evenly spaced around the walls. The ceiling was high with large, heavy beams exposed, and the walls were a type of plaster or stucco with what looked like natural grain stalks mixed into it. The whole look was that of a medieval building, in both materials and construction.

The doors were of varied styles and materials from long ago to present and there was one that looked like it could be from the future. The doors went in a progression from old to new as if it were the intended order, in Cameron's mind, for investigating them.

"Shall we start with oldest to newest?" he asked, attempting to prove his confidence.

The futuristic-looking door was to their right and had no door handle or any visible means of opening it while the oldest looking one was just to their left. It was made from old wood and had a red cross crudely painted on it with the words, "Lord; have mercy on us" inscribed. There were large stone blocks on either side and over the top of it. Above four of the doorways there were dates inscribed. The door with the cross had 1665-1666 for its dates. Next was a door made of wood but older than modern times. It had the date 1918 above it. The next one had a door that looked very much like it belonged to a red and white airplane with the date 1959, and the last one with a date was metal painted gray with the year 1983 over it.

The last three doors had the words "Yesterday," "Today," and "Tomorrow" written above them. Each one was unique for its designation of time. The first was a simple wooden door with a white glass doorknob like doors used to have in the 50s or 60s, the next one was a lot like the one on Cameron's house and the last one had no doorknob or visible means of opening it. You couldn't tell if it opened from the right or left or from the top down or bottom up.

"It might open like the ones you see in science fiction movies with a swoosh sound," said Cameron. "I guess we'll have to wait and see."

Between all of the doors, except for the oldest and newest, there were switches on the wall. The switch handle was set in a triangle pattern with the top position labeled 'natural' and the bottom two points labeled 'edit' to the left and 'engage' to the right. You were able to move the switch from 'natural' to 'edit' and from 'edit' to 'engage,' depending on which choice you made.

"Let me explain how this works, Cam," said Sonja. "Each of the four doors with dates over them have scenarios that are based on real events in history. As you experience each one, you are given a choice to either engage right away or edit the scenario; then you come out and take a look through the 'yesterday' door to see if you want to engage what you have edited. You have the power to revise history, sound fun?"

"So, I do go from oldest to newest than, right?" asked Cameron.

"After each edit, you can see the results by going through the 'yesterday' door and experience what effect, if any, your edit had on the future," said Sonja. "The 'today' door is only used if you are pleased with how things went and didn't edit any of the scenarios. Once you enter it, you are stuck with your decision, no going back, and you will be scored accordingly. The 'tomorrow' door is a mystery until all of your edits have been engaged and locked in. You can go into the 'yesterday' door to see the consequences of your edits, but not until all of your choices are engaged will you be allowed to enter the 'tomorrow' door. It's an exit holding room, as well where you will receive your score for the edit choices you made."

"Okay, now it sounds fun, shall we begin?" asked Cameron eagerly. "This is a game that I can get into!"

"So, I know that you think that it will be like playing a game, although not as interactive as most, and I want you to feel that way, but you need to take it a little more seriously too," said Sonja. "After all, these decisions will have an impact on you, even if they won't on the real world as you know it now. It used to be that we didn't let any of the edits be viewed until the scenarios were engaged. This is an upgrade to the training program. I don't know if I like it as much. People need to take ownership of the decisions they make, don't you think?"

"Well, it's not like it's going to change reality, right? I mean, it's nice to be able to see the results of our decisions so that we can make adjustments," Cameron said.

"But that's what I was saying, you need to take it more seriously than that," she said with exasperation. "In life we don't have that option. We have to think things through and consider the consequences of our actions. The outcome of our decisions can have devastating results. People have to take responsibility for their actions. That is the way worlds benefit from wisdom."

They stood in front of the old wooden door with the red cross painted on it and the words "Lord, have mercy on us" and pushed it open. They found themselves in an old English town square in the village of Eyam. Words suspended in the air above the square. They read: 'The Village of Eyam, Derbyshire, August 30, 1665, population—344.' There was a horse-drawn cart coming down the narrow, cobblestone street. The driver stopped in front of the tailor shop that was across the street from them and climbed down off the horse. He took a large box full of material off the cart and carried it into the shop.

"What are we supposed to do now, Sonja? Just stand here and watch?" asked Cameron. "Not much going on."

"No, we can *sit* and watch," she said, motioning toward a bench.

They sat and waited for a few minutes, and the scene began to change. It got all blurry as the interior of the tailor's shop came into focus.

"Alexander, here are the cloth samples from London that you ordered," said the driver as he set the large box on the counter.

"Thank you, George," said Alexander as he looked through the box. "These things are soaking wet and musty smelling; you will have to take them home and set them out to dry before we can do anything with them."

The voices began to get softer as a haze started to fill the air.

"I will take them, then," said George. "Would you mind if I used some of the patterns in the meantime?"

The images slowly faded as well and words came up to reveal, "The Home of George Vickers—September 3, 1665". They saw a family surrounding a bed where George lay dying.

Next, there were images of other households digging graves in their front and back yards, dragging family members out of houses with red crosses painted on the doors. The plague was taking its toll on the village of Eyam.

There were scenes of food being brought to a place called Mompesson's Well, named after the village rector, William. He and his assistant admonished the townsfolk not to cross a certain boundary surrounding the village, designated by large stone and mound landmarks. It was at the Boundary Stone and Mompesson's Well where outsiders would quickly leave food and medical supplies. Money for the food was left and taken from a small pool of vinegar because the people thought that the germs of the plague would be washed off the coins this way.

There was one scene where William Mompesson was preaching in the open air on a rock in a dell. "Summer is upon us. I am closing the Eyam Parish Church to worshippers, for fear that the hot weather will make things worse. Instead, we will meet in this outdoor enclave we will call Cucklett Church. We shall gather here to pray twice a week and hold our Sunday service here."

He persuaded the villagers not to flee and spread the infection, but to stay until the plague had run its course. Next, they saw the tombstone of his wife, Catherine, one of the many plague victims, in the Eyam churchyard.

Suddenly, the scene began to turn hazy and there came the words across the sky, rolling up like the end credits after a movie: "After mid-October 1666, the deaths ceased. Of the 344 villagers in Eyam, 259 died this horrible plague death, including 58 children. November 20, 1666: 'Our town has become a Golgotha, the place of a skull; and had there not been a small remnant left, we had been as Sodom, and like to Gomorrah. My ears never heard such doleful lamentations—my nose never smelled such horrid smells, and my eyes never beheld such ghastly spectacles.'"

For sure, this charming, peaceful village—then regarded as the valley of death—was hell on earth.

The plague, caused by a bacterium, hits its victims with fever, chills, vomiting, headaches, diarrhea and delirium. Symptoms include a rosy, red rash, and black boils (from dried blood under the skin, caused by internal bleeding) appear in the armpits, neck and groin. The "Black Death," as it is known, can be excruciatingly painful and horrible for others to watch.

What makes this bucolic, mountainous Derbyshire village (known as the Plague Town) so unique is not only that the plague wiped out such a high number of residents in such a short time, but also the way that its devastated townsfolk reacted to the deadly, infectious disease. It was because of this self-enforced isolation that the plague did not spread to surrounding areas. They sacrificed themselves so others could live; courageously cordoning themselves off from the outside world, the Eyam villagers kept the evil event from spreading further, and this was the last place it hit in England.

As they got up to leave, Sonja said, “The whole incident might not have happened if that box of samples had not been brought from London. How would you like to set the switch? It’s all up to you. Then we can move along to the next door.”

“If I choose to edit the scenario, would it get rid of the delivery?” asked Cameron.

“That’s what I would imagine, but you would have to put the switch in the edit position and then check the ‘yesterday’ door to try and find out if the change made any difference to the good or to the bad,” said Sonja. “If the consequences change to your liking, you can move the switch into the engage position and it’s locked in. There’s no going back once this is done.”

Cameron thought a little about that and asked, “If I choose to edit this out of history, would any of the other three have changes based on the edited outcome of this scenario?”

“That’s the chance that you have to take, and when each edit is engaged, the results can be viewed through the ‘tomorrow’ door, which will become our exit door when all of the scenario edits are engaged,” said Sonja. “If you choose not to engage in any of the edits, we can leave through the ‘today’ door, but then all you would have done is watch a history lesson.”

"Well, I can't imagine that it would only have the consequence of the delivery being made; it might have the consequence of more people being killed by changing their demeanor to not care about the outside world, and the plague would have spread further. I just don't know," Cameron puzzled. "I choose not to edit the scenario." And with that, Cameron placed the switch in the engage position. "On to the next door, Sonja."

They stepped over to the next wooden door with the date 1918 over top and tried to open it. It gave a little resistance but swung free with a little coaxing and a loud squeak. The scene was of a busy street in Salt Lake City, Utah. It was around dusk, and there was an old-style, wheeled newspaper stand down the road with the late edition just coming in. The bundles were thrown off a delivery truck, and as they were being put out, Cameron bought one and read the headlines trying to get a clue as to what the scenario was trying to show him.

The headline read: *"Influenza Is Spreading Fast Here, twenty-five new cases reported."* Part of the main article read: *"On the afternoon of October 4, the Salt Lake City Board of Health met to discuss the small number of influenza cases that had been discovered in the city and to decide what action to take to try to stop the disease from spreading. The Board believed that there were eight to ten cases, all spread from a family from Wyoming that had come to attend the state fair."*

As they read down through the page, there was an article bolded that said: *"One of the youngest to succumb to the flu virus thus far, at only twelve years of age, Louis S. Goodman died at Judge Mercy Hospital early this afternoon."* The words were almost glowing, as if to get their attention. If it were not for the blatant position of the news stand, and all of the people milling about and blending into the background as if in faded-out background footage of an old movie, they would have thought that there was something more to the scenario, but they both looked at each other and knew that that was it.

"I don't know who this Louis S. Goodman was, but do you think that it will become obvious if I were to edit the scenario?" Cameron asked Sonja. "I can't see that there is any more to this story unless it is like the last one, and we see what plays out when the flu spreads. I don't recall this epidemic from history classes in school."

"I think that would be a safe assumption. We can exit, and you can edit the scenario and see what it's all about," said Sonja.

"I'm almost sure that this young boy will be spared in the edit, but what if he turns out to be a serial killer or some other kind of monster?" Cameron asked. "I would rather he turn out to be some rich benefactor for the cause of wiping out poverty or something good for a change."

Upon leaving, Cameron pulled the switch into the edit position and they walked over to the "yesterday" door. There were some odd sounds and funny lights pulsing around the door frame, and then they were allowed to open it. As they entered, all was dark at first. The scene began to lighten up to reveal the dawn with the sunrise sky reflecting in the Great Salt Lake. From a vantage point above the city, the scene dropped down to street level, and there was a newer newspaper stand and they knew that the time was more modern. The headline of the morning edition was: *"University of Utah College of Medicine's Chairman of Pharmacology and Physiology uses Curare for Surgical Relaxant."* It went on to tell about how Professor Louis S. Goodman along with Dr. Alfred Gilman pioneered the first chemotherapy trials. The date on the newspaper was 1944.

"So, according to this, Louis eventually gets together with Alfred and they come up with chemotherapy which has saved over a half million lives since this newspaper came out. That is worth editing history for, wouldn't you say, Cam?"

"I think that I will engage this edit," reasoned Cameron. "It seems like a no-brainer to me too."

"It would appear that the outcome had nothing to do with the influenza epidemic that swept across the country in 1918 and 1919. Unlike the first scenario," said Sonja. "It's interesting to note that although Goodman moved to Salt Lake City in 1944, he was born in Portland, Oregon, and moved to various states before settling there as the Chairman and Professor of Pharmacology at the new, four-year University of Utah College of Medicine."

Leaving the "yesterday" room, Cameron went straight over and put the switch for room number 1918 into the "engage" position. There was a mechanical sound as if the workings of editing time were from some kind of huge steampunk machine. He figured that it was only for effect in the game-like scenario, even if Sonja told him not to think of them as such.

"Well, that sounds like that is that. Are we ready to move on to the next door?" Cameron asked with a little tinge of anticipation in his voice. "These doors are like opening up presents on Christmas morning. I wish there were more than just four."

"It sounds like you were given quite a lot at Christmas. Did your brother get as much as you?" asked Sonja.

"Yes, he did," said Cameron. "But it's not like we were spoiled growing up. We had our troubles and struggles. You, no doubt, love to get presents the same as I do, right?"

"That's beside the point. This is not about me. There are real stories that take serious consideration behind these doors. It's not only a game," said Sonja.

"Regardless, Sonja, I can't wait to open the next door. I mean, look at it. Painted white and red like Christmas wrapping paper!" said Cameron. "1959 was a little before my time but not as far before my time as 1665 and 1918 were."

Stepping up to the door, Cameron grabbed the handle to an airplane and pulled it open. They were in Clear Lake, Iowa, according to the text that floated above the scene. There was a marquee with the title "Winter Dance Party Featuring Buddy Holly, Ritchie Valens and the 'Big Bopper', J.P. Richardson." Before they could go into the theater, the scene changed with a mist that quickly formed and dissipated into snow. It was cold, and the scene was of a corn field in the middle of the night. A storm was raging.

"Boy, this is quite a blizzard! I can barely see my hand in front of my face," Cameron said as they both tried to find something to focus on. As with the other rooms, the door and walls faded and there was a bench in relatively the same spot, left of where the door had been. They decided not to sit as it was much too cold; they needed to keep their arms and legs moving to try and stay warm. They stood, walking in place for a while, until they heard the sound of an engine overhead and above the squall of the storm winds. Lights began to flicker through the driving snow in the sky and off to their left.

"Too low, it's too low," Cameron yelled above the noise. "That's a plane, and it's going to crash, I know it is!"

Just then the roaring blur of an aircraft came careening down at a grotesque angle and smashed into the ground of the corn field across Interstate I-35 from where the two were standing. They forgot that they were cold and ran over to the wrecked plain. As their eyes adjusted to the dark and through the smoke, Cameron could read the registration number N3794N along the back of the body of the craft.

"This was the aircraft that carried rock-n-roll stars Buddy Holly, Ritchie Valens and the 'Big Bopper' to their death in a corn field on February 3, 1959. What would your history be like if he or the others had never died?" asked Sonja.

"So, it wasn't my kind of music since I was born much later into much different kinds of music, but I can see how a lot of people would have loved to see what they would have come up with next. I just can't see the need to change this part of history. Besides, I heard somewhere that his wife had a miscarriage and couldn't attend his funeral. Now I'm not sure if it was because of his death or not, but I think it's fitting to not have Buddy experience that at least, don't you?"

"Well, it's all up to you, so what are you going to do?"

As they left the room back through the airplane door, Cameron said, "I choose not to edit this scenario." Then he put the switch in the "engage" position and started for the fourth and final door.

"Well, we can't change that now, but weren't you the least interested in what new songs Buddy Holly would have come up with?"

"Maybe you're right," Cameron said. "I should have done an edit first, but I guess that I wanted to take the serious approach. It's not going to happen in real life anyway, so why tease? Plus, it's not the kind of music I care about."

“That’s right, you like that alternative music. I like cool jazz,” Sonja said as they walked away from the airplane door. “So, one more left. Are you ready for it?”

They stood in front of a heavy door which looked like it belonged to a bunker of some sort. Made of iron with a large locking arm across the middle, there was a large wheel that could be turned, allowing the locked arm to be drawn up and to swing inward so that the large door opened with a controlled motion almost effortlessly. They stepped into a room that had banks of instruments and old-style computers with lights snapping on and clicking off. Occasionally, there would be a paper readout regurgitated from a console, dot matrix style. There were several scientists in lab coats standing around, reading the dials and monitoring instruments.

One in particular was sitting at a desk with the name plaque that read, ‘Lieutenant Colonel Stanislav Petros—Soviet Union Air Defense Forces.’ He was watching a computer monitor that suddenly turned red with the word “launch” flashing on it as a siren started to howl. The man just sat staring at it for a few seconds.

They positioned themselves on a bench that was situated in roughly the same relative place as in the other scenarios and watched. The date, 26 September 1983, hovered over the scene and slowly faded away.

"Colonel Petros, these sensors are indicating that missiles have been launched towards us," said one of the scientists. "They have detected an incoming missile strike from the United States."

Another said, with urgency in his voice, "The computer readouts are suggesting that several missiles have been launched. Colonel, must I remind you that it's your job to register apparent enemy missile launches? We must begin returning fire."

"There was no rule about how long I am allowed to think before reporting," Stanislav responded. The siren howled, but he just sat there for a few seconds, staring at the big, back-lit, red screen with the word "launch" on it. He sensed that something was amiss. A minute later the siren went off again. The second missile was launched. Then the third, and the fourth, and the fifth. Computers changed their alerts from "launch" to "missile strike."

"Protocol states that we should respond to a nuclear attack with one of our own," the other men barked at him.

"The nature of the alert seems to be abundantly clear, but I am suspicious of just how strong and clear the alert is. I have some doubts." Petrov called the duty officer in the Soviet army's headquarters and reported a system malfunction. If he was wrong, the first nuclear explosions would have happened minutes later. Twenty-three minutes later and nothing happened.

"If there had been a real strike, then we would already know about it. It is such a relief that the awful repercussions for the world have been averted," he said with a smile. "You are lucky I was on shift tonight. I am the only officer in this team that received a civilian education. You, my dear colleagues, are all professional soldiers. You were taught to give and obey orders without hesitation," he told them. "If somebody else had been on shift, the alarm would have been raised."

The whole scene faded down, indicating that the scenario was concluded. Cameron and Sonja got up and headed for the door. As they left the room, Cameron reached over and positioned the switch to engage without saying a word.

"You would be amazed at how many engaged the edit for Stanislav Petrov to retaliate with a nuclear attack just to see how a nuclear disaster like that would affect the world. Curiosity killed more than the cat; it also killed their chances for being chosen for the program," said Sonja. "And it makes me wonder if saving the earth with people like them in it is a worthwhile thing to do. Of course, I'm kidding, but we have to completely erase their minds of having any recollections of the program whatsoever."

Walking over to the "tomorrow" door, having all of the switches in the engage positions, the door parted open from the middle with a Star Trek swoosh.

"I knew that it would sound like that—cool!" Cameron said as they walked in to see a kind of control-paneled theater room with a large view screen at one end.

"Boy, it sure doesn't take much for your nerd switch to be flipped, does it?" Sonja joked while the numbers were coming into focus on the screen. "So here we are in the results room. And it looks like you have earned 38%. Wow, that's impressive, Cam."

In the next room before the exit, they found themselves in the studio workshop of Leonardo DaVinci. His drawings, paintings, sculpture and scale models for a wide variety of inventions were strewn about like a little kid's room that desperately needed to be cleaned up and the toys put away.

"'Once you have tasted flight, you will forever walk on the earth with your eyes turned skyward, for there you have been, and there you will always long to return.' Leonardo da Vinci said that," said Sonja.

"Museums allow us to see man at the high points and the low points of his history," she added "Things that were known have been forgotten but things that are remembered can be brought into the new light of today and find function. What is it that man is trying to accomplish in the world? Have we forgotten? Can we find some clues here in the museum?"

"I see them as places to gather food for thought," said Cameron. "I heard somewhere that there is nothing new under the sun, but if we are to improve the condition of the world, there must be something that was lacking in the first iteration of these things that we look back on in awe."

“There is food for health, as well as taste,” said Sonja. “Throughout history we have types of clothing, for comfort, warmth, as well as style. It seems that everything is pointing to entertainment, fun and games and sports.” She turned to face Camron, looking serious. "Mankind has forgotten that people need each other. Two of the other scenarios in the cave in the woods that went fleetingly by when you were waiting for your score were of Christians being held to be fed to hungry lions if they didn’t renounce their belief in God. Would you be willing to die for what you believe in? The other one was of a cave converted into a fancy restaurant for the enjoyment of the filthy rich. Funny how the same venue can have so many different usages, but it all comes down to food and clothing.”

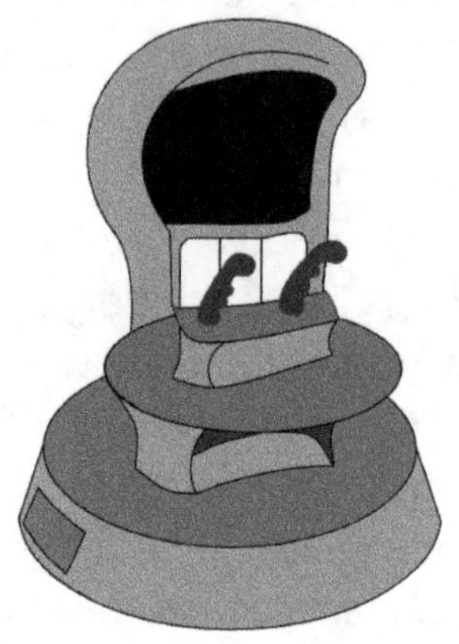

Chapter Five:

The Mall

The day started out just like a Saturday used to. Cameron was able to sleep in and get up to his favorite routine of a leisurely breakfast with whoever was left home (his mom and Chuck for a change) and a little TV time before he took Sandy out for a walk and to play in the yard. He noticed how long the grass was getting and decided to mow it.

He headed in with Sandy, and when he turned to close the door, he noticed Sonja had followed him in. She startled him as he turned around and saw her. Chuck was sitting on the couch with his guitar, and his mom was coming through the living room with a basket of dirty laundry.

"Hi Cam! What are your plans for today?" asked Sonja.

Chuck and his mom went about their business as Cameron turned to answer her.

"I have the lawn to mow and I'm gonna go online with my friends later, the usual," said Cameron. "Why? Did you have another mind bender to take me on?"

"Oh, I was just wondering if you wanted to go to the mall. I need some new shoes, and it's slim pickings around here," she said. "The shoe stores here don't have what I'm looking for."

"Well, if you can come back in about an hour, I will have the lawn done and can be ready to go with you, although I don't know why you need me to go with you," said Cameron.

Sonja pulled up in front of Cameron's house in an old Toyota about an hour and a half later. Cameron came out and got in the car, and they were off.

"You have to get me back before our game tonight," Cameron said. "I still don't see why you have to drag me along. You can get any kind of shoes your heart could possibly desire online. I'm not one of those mall goers. It just doesn't thrill me"

"Where's your sense of adventure, the thrill of the hunt? Come on, it will be fun," Sonja assured him. "Besides, we have a lesson today that I think you will love."

"What could you possibly pair up with the mall for a scenario of instruction?" Cameron asked. "You used a cave in the woods, an alien invasion for the zoo, the Museum made sense with how the past can be useful to give future direction, but the mall? This could be interesting."

"Cam, just think of the mall as the modern-day center of commerce. Such a wide variety of goods brought together in one place just for us. Everything you might need all in one place. Or just a place to meet with your friends and hang out plus a realized habitat for the endangered mall walker of the species," said Sonja.

"You are weird," Cameron shot back.

The remainder of the trip was mostly uneventful, other than fighting over which radio station to listen to. Sonja was more into cool jazz, and Cameron liked the alternative stations.

Thirty-five minutes later Sonja parked along the street in front of a community center and got out. She looked in the window before going in. Cameron followed with a question on his mind.

"What are we doing, Sonja?"

"I just wanted to see what was available in here. Look, you can play pool or football, and there are tables to play your board games and card games on. There is a clothes closet, a food pantry; as well as that, a bulletin board with job listings, volunteer opportunities and services for help with homework, getting loans and grants and scholarships for school, also a driver's training course. What a deal! There's even a daycare service for infants and toddlers. I bet the mall doesn't have all that," said Sonja.

"Yes, but why come in here; what does it have that you need?" asked Cameron. "I doubt if you want to buy a pair of used shoes from here. There are some older arcade games over there, though."

"Is that all you ever talk about or notice here? This is a community-centered center, and a lot of it is free. They want to help you out with money and things, not clean you out of money with expensive things," said Sonja, scolding him. "Let's get going to the mall."

They parked in the front of what used to be Sears and went in through the main entrance just to the left of it. The kiosk with the layout of the mall was down the hall just before the first intersection of hallways and the railing to look over down to the lower level.

"Eastfield Mall, quite the place for being so old, fifty-two years. It was built in early 1967 with three anchor stores; JC Penney, Macy's and Sears. They closed in 2011, 2016 and 2018, respectively," said Sonja. "But it does have a sixteen-screen theater."

"Who are you all of a sudden, a walking, talking version of

Wikipedia?" Cameron said. "How is it that you know so much about this mall thirty miles from Ware?"

Cameron wasn't really expecting an answer; she most likely had looked it up online.

"In here, we have such a variety of things; anything you could ever want. We don't have to travel to the far away countries where the things are made; it is all brought here for us. Everything in one place. Or we can just hang-out and eat in the food court or in one of the fancy expensive restaurants," she said.

"What did you want to come here for again? You know that we can get anything we need in Ware, and anything else we can order online?" said Cameron.

"To get out. Don't you just want to get out once in a while?" she shot back. "In some cultures of the world, there would be grand marketplaces to which tribes would bring their wares to sell. The mall is our modern-day counterpart to that. Interstate commerce and all that."

"Did you do a report on this for school or something? Your way too into it," said Cameron. "I thought you wanted to go to Footaction for shoes. I'll be at the Arcade if that's where you're going."

"Oh, come on, don't you have any imagination? Just think of each new store as a different country's wares brought here at great peril and purpose over stormy seas; in order to sustain its people, the trade goods that are exchanged so they can survive the coming, harsh winter," Sonja dramatically proclaimed.

"Sometimes I think you're just plain nuts," replied Cameron. "Do you want to get something to eat and go see a movie or something?"

"That sounds like something two people would do on a date. Is this a date, Cam?" asked Sonja.

"Do you want it to be a date?" asked Cameron, regretting his words the minute he asked.

"You want it to be a date. Even though your parents wouldn't approve of your dating at your young age," she said. "But it can be our little secret, if you can play along with some ideas that I have in mind for you."

"Now that has me worried, you see, because my friends already see us as husband and wife and ... what do you mean ideas you have in mind for me?" Cameron asked with confusion. "Why do I get the impression that you know me better than you could know me?"

"Would your friends say anything to your parents about our relationship?" asked Sonja, side-stepping his question. "In real time, outside of the venues, I am two years older than you."

"No, definitely not, and as far as I know, they wouldn't have any reason to. Why?" he asked.

"Nothing, it's just that they might be starting to see changes in you, your behavior," she said.

"Well, it's too late for that; they already have," said Cameron with a sigh. "They think that I am finally off my meds."

"What? You're on medication?" asked Sonja excitedly. "I was led to believe that you were perfectly healthy."

"No, it's just that now they see me coming out of my cave more often than usual," explained Cameron. "Seriously though, how do you know so much about this mall? You just moved to Ware three months ago."

"Well, I don't know what stores are in it altogether," Sonja replied, as she edged around the question. "Let's explore."

"Let's get something to eat," he said. "Then we can explore."

They settled for Yum Yum Kitchen for lunch. It was set up cafeteria style, and they both ordered the same turkey club sandwich with chips and tomato juice. Cameron went through the line first, so he thought that Sonja was just copying him. She insisted that she wasn't, but he doubted that. She also insisted on paying for his meal, as well as hers, to which he didn't protest too much as he made very little with his lawn mowing jobs for his neighbors.

They sat and made small talk for a while as they had their

lunch, and when they finished, they just sat for a little while more. There was a relationship beginning to grow. As much as Cameron didn't want to admit it, he was falling for her.

"So, seriously, where do you want to go in this mall?" asked Cameron.

"So, seriously, I want to go to Footaction for a new pair of shoes," she replied. "You can go to your dumb old arcade, and I will meet you there when I'm finished."

"That sounds like a plan that I can get behind. I'll see you in a while," said Cameron as he took up all of the trash from their lunch and walked off toward the exit.

When he dumped the tray into the garbage receptacle at the exit, he noticed a small gem-like item slip from it. He was fortunate to be able to retrieve it from the top of all the trash in the bin. Thinking that it had to be Sonja's, he put it in his pocket for safe keeping. Sonja had already gone off to the shoe store, so he started to head for the arcade.

When he got there, the first thing he did was collect ten dollars' worth of tokens for the games and then sought out his favorites. Some of them were from way back but there were a few up-to-date consoles as well. After dropping $4.50 worth into the Galaga and Centipede, he spotted a new one that he had never seen before. Spotted it, because it seemed to vanish when he took a few steps back to pick up a token that he dropped. It might have been his imagination, given all the crazy things that were going on in his life lately, but he was almost sure that it faded out for a few seconds.

The name of the game was *Alpha Generate* and he had never even heard of it before. The graphics were very cool, almost three dimensional on the panels and sides. The controls were very ergonomically fit for his hands as if it were made for him specifically. As he stood there with the controls in hand, he looked everywhere for the token slot but couldn't find one. Enjoying the feel of the controls, he started to gaze at the artwork and became mesmerized by it. His head started to spin, and he found himself being drawn into the game as if it were one of the light gates. Suddenly, with a blinding white flash that melded into the scene, he was inside the game.

"What in the world?" he said out loud. "How could this happen? Sonja isn't even here!"

He realized that it most likely had to do with the green gemstone that he put in his pocket back in the food court. That must be how Sonja activated the light gates, he thought. But what could this place teach me? It looks like a sci-fi, outer space mall.

He looked around and had the feeling that nobody even noticed that he was there. He looked at his hands and arms and noticed that there was hardly a change to his appearance as a virtual player in this scenario. There were plenty of people or beings around; it's just that they were all going about their own business without giving him any notice whatsoever. He was sure that if he interacted with them that they would interact with him, but for now he just wanted to be an observer. He was also a little afraid, not knowing what was expected of him in this strange new environment.

A loud announcement came over a speaker placed in the large opening in the square of storefronts he found himself in.

"Trelic Blue, your package has arrived in compartment Zed seven. You have twelve nantz to pick it up. Trelic Blue, your package has arrived in compartment Zed seven. You have twelve nantz to pick it up."

Just then, an enormously tall being dressed in tight fitting clothes came running across the floor, nearly slipping and falling, to get a cube wrapped in shiny, purple cloth that had just dropped into a trough with the letter Z and the number 7 branded along its side. Cameron didn't know how long a nantz was, but apparently it was less than a second based on the frantic pace that Trelic Blue took to get his package.

Cameron watched for a while as Trelic made his way down a wide hallway and out an archway that flickered a hazy yellow orange. As he followed him through, it tickled a little, and the terrain on the other side was totally different from what he perceived as some kind of futuristic mall that he just stepped out of.

It was nighttime here, and the stars were bright against a blue galactic cloud with very vivid colors and swirling details that made him think that he was looking at one of those high-definition telescope images. It was striking, distracting to the point of Cameron losing track of Trelic as he went down a street of dwellings. He didn't know which one he could have ducked into.

As Cameron slowed his pace and looked up at the sky, wondering where Trelic went, he began to look side to side until something caught his eye. Between two of the dwellings, in a backyard, he saw Trelic unwrapping the package that he had retrieved from the bin back at the mall. As he got closer to see what it was, and what Trelic was doing with it, he saw that it looked like some kind of electronic modular piece of a sci-fi Rube Goldberg machine.

The part had a lens in the top of it, and when Trelic snapped it into place, there was a whirring sound followed by crimson smoke curling up off selected sections of a menagerie of pipe-looking connections and other bizarre modular moving parts to conclude in a beam of light that shot up through the night sky. There was a loud noise of what Cameron thought sounded like applause and a giant number *37%* projected in laser lights.

Cameron came from between the two dwellings to reveal himself to Trelic.

"Hi, Trelic Blue. My name is Cameron Adams. Can we talk?" asked Cameron.

Trelic twisted around to Cameron, so startled that he almost fell over. "Why did you follow me? Who are you?" Trelic asked. "I got the elements fair and square. That is a legitimate score."

"I am just a human from Earth, and I want to learn how you go about entering the competition. What do I have to do?" Cameron asked with slight hesitation. "Do I need money to enter?"

"You need more than money; you need courage, time and patience," Trelic explained. "I am done with this part and so will move on. You can get a game sheet from the Prefect at Guum. The first one is free. Now, I must go, for here comes my shuttle."

A sleek-looking craft landed silently beside the large, tall being, and not believing his eyes, Cameron saw it get inside even though he was sure that the craft was too small for him. Then the shuttle was off as silently as it had arrived.

Cameron thought that Guum must be the square that he had just left, so he walked back to see if there was a Prefect there. As he made his way back up the street that he had chased Trelic down, he noticed a lot more than when he was in pursuit. There were weird animals that had pieces missing from their bodies, but they were still alive, running around as if nothing was wrong with them. The beings that he encountered along the way were also strange. No two were alike, as if they were all from different species or planets. Cameron tried to talk to some of them, but they ran off scared, as if he would hurt them.

The archway that flickered a hazy yellow orange when Cameron went through it the first time had the word, *Guum* over the top of it on this side, and as he went through it to get back to the square, he felt the same tickle and noticed the change from the terrain of the town to that of the mall. He felt like he was inside and that there was a ceiling overhead as he proceeded to the square, but it was more of a sense of being inside than actually being in a building. A feeling of protection and not being vulnerable.

Back in the square, Cameron noticed more detail in the storefronts, as well. The Prefect was one of the more prominent edifices in the square. He walked up to the window that looked like a ticket booth at the Prefect storefront and asked a rather large-faced man for a game card.

“This yur firstly?” asked the man.

“Yes, it is, and I’m not sure how to play. Could you direct me to someone that could help with that?” asked Cameron. “I tried to get Trelic Blue’s help, but he left.”

“No reason fur him to stick iff it were fins, I recon,” he said. “There may be hep along th’way.”

Cameron took the card and found a place to sit and read what was involved in the game. The first thing he noticed was large writing at the bottom. It read,“Place blood sample here,” with an arrow pointing to a circle in the lower right corner. Odd, he thought, but what would it hurt?

The text was simple enough. There was a place for his name, his age and planet of origin and a fill-in asking, "Why are
you here?"

"That one's simple, to win the game," he said out loud. There were seven components needed to assemble the beacon plus the light lens that you must order as soon as your color was known. Your color would be assigned as soon as you offer your blood sample and turn in this card. Then there was a list of what the seven components were with a place to mark them off when they were found and placed in the contraption.

1. Base
2. Mixer/ Elixirs
3. Tubes
4. Combiner
5. Top Seat
6. Holalectrum
7. Lens

'Well, this might just be impossible. I don't have a clue,' Cameron said to himself.

Just then he noticed smaller print that began with "Clues." The first one in the list corresponded to the first item on the list of components. It said, "Base—best of five on Alpha Generate."

"Okay, now I'm getting someplace. That was the name of the game that got me into this mess. Where could it have gone?"

Cameron looked around for the game and noticed an arcade-type game room a few doors down from the Prefect's window. Then he remembered that he had to turn in his game card with the blood sample on it in order to get his color. Did that have anything to do with the last piece, the lens?

He wasn't quite sure, so he got his pocket knife out and pricked his finger. He pressed the blood that he squeezed up onto the card in the circle and went to the Prefect's window and asked, "Is this just for my color, or do I have time to get the pieces before the lens arrives?"

The Prefect didn't answer him but took the card and inserted it into a slot in a terminal behind him. Instantly he had the results. He handed it back and his name had the word "Gamboge" added to it. Trelic Blue, Cameron Gamboge.

"What kind of color is gamboge?" he said out loud.

But just as he spoke, he noticed that a patch of color had been added after his name. It was a yellow mustard color, a little bit darker than normal. He still wasn't sure if he needed all of the pieces to the contraption first before he turned it in, but it was too late now. He had to work the clues, and the first one was a competition on a video game. That should be easy, he thought.

Cameron walked into the arcade and found the Alpha Generate console sitting on a round, raised platform. When he approached the game, the disk floor began to turn slowly. He got his bearings and focused on the game screen. There was no need for a token, the game started as soon as he took hold of the ergonomic controls.

Stages One of Five came up on the screen in old-school, pixelated graphics of a crane loading a truck with something that was the same color as on the game card, gamboge. As he controlled the loading and then switched to driving the truck away from the loading site, little ant-like creatures started to attack the truck and take parts of the load. There was a button that he hadn't tried yet, and it turned out to be guns that came out of the sides of the truck to repel the bugs. The road that he was driving on had twists and turns until, finally, he came to a dock at an ocean with a large ship in port. As he continued to repel the bugs, he maneuvered the truck along the moorings, and another crane began taking the gamboge-colored stuff from the truck and loading the ship.

The load on the ship needed to be at a minimum level, and just one truck load was not enough. Cameron thought that if he could get one more load and keep the bugs off completely, he would have enough for a full load in the ship. With skills from a long history of gaming, Cameron was able to get the next load fully loaded into the ship, resulting in a victory screen that faded quickly into the next chapter. The graphics also changed, a little more modern but not quite HD CG yet. That would be himself in this scenario simulation.

The next stage of the game was taking the ship over the sea to another land to unload it. There had to be enough left to unload or he would have to go back and get more. With the controls firmly understood, Cameron was confident that he could do it in one trip. As he headed out to sea, there were giant birdlike creatures that he had to fend off and monsters from the water that resembled giant octopuses and whale-like creatures. The hardest ones were the little, tiny fish that would come flying up out of the water and grab a nibble from time to time. In the end, he arrived with more than enough to satisfy the quota for phase two of the game, and he again, got the victory screen.

The next two phases of the game were increasingly more modern in both graphics and the gameplay controls. Phase Three was getting the ship unloaded while zombies and a giant behemoth from the deep attacked. The trucks got more detailed and better guns, but the monsters were harder as well, just like with any game leveling up.

Phase Four had nice graphics and smooth controls as Cameron distributed the gamboge to points around a city in exotic cars like in some of the new racing games. There were police chases and roadblocks, unbelievable jumps over drawbridges and tunnels of terror but he got all the gamboge to their respective locations in time and with plenty to spare.

The last phase, Phase Five, was delivering the gamboge to the same place where he received the game card. It was perhaps one of the easiest phases of the game, and he couldn't understand why. He was all ready for the game of his life, so to speak, but even the graphics reverted back to the way they were in Phase One. He soon realized that the difficulty level went up throughout all of the phases, and if the player did well enough through to Phase Five, they were awarded the best score and the easiest level for the final phase. The strangest thing was that the game avatar that hand-delivered the gamboge to the Prefect looked undeniably like Cameron.

The game was over, and the disk that sat in the middle of the arcade slowed its spinning. Cameron hadn't noticed that with each phase it would speed up a little, evidence of how focused he was playing the game. But now he felt a little dizzy as he stepped down into a large crowd that he also hadn't noticed gathering during his game. They were cheering and making all kinds of strange sounding noises that Cameron was not familiar with, as everyone was from some different race or planet. His victory screen was showing up on all the video screens in the place with a score of one million. He heard someone in the crowd saying that it was the highest the score was designed to reach on the game.

The noise from the crowd changed slightly as everyone began to "ooh" and "aah." Cameron looked at the dais where the game sat motionless as a door opened in the base of it. There was the first item from the list, the base component for the contraption that he was supposed to construct. He took the box that had the base in it and left the arcade to sit on one of the benches. He had to know what the next clue was for the second item, the mixer. The clue said, 'Mixer: Socialize with four races, ask the write questions.' Cameron thought that there must be a mistake on the spelling of 'write' until he realized that it might be the questions that he answered on the game card. He needed to get their names, their ages and planets of origin and ask why they were here. That sounded easy enough; there were all kinds of 'people' in this place.

Cameron looked at some of the other clues before he would start to round up the four individuals for the 'mixer'. One was for 'the combiner.' 'Whatever that is,' he thought. Cameron was thinking that he had to hurry with collecting the parts because he didn't know when the lens would be ordered or when it would arrive, so he tried to figure out the clue for the combiner as well. He read, 'Combiner: Clearly the color becomes a parent.'

As Cameron sat there puzzling over the clue, there came a small person who sat down beside him.

"Do you need help with that?" the small person said. Cameron wasn't sure what the small person's gender was or what world it might have come from.

"No, well, yes. Thank you. It's this clue. Have you played the game before?" asked Cameron.

"Many times. My name is Ebsar. I am pleased to be of service to you," it said. Cameron was no closer to figuring out their gender by that name, so he introduced himself.

"My name is Cameron, I'm from Earth," Cameron said.

"Well, excuse my bluntness, but are you male or female? I can't tell from your name," said Ebsar. "It will help to not be awkward when we get to know each other better."

"I totally understand. As a matter of fact, I am not quite sure of your gender either. I am male of my species," said Cameron thinking that he should never have to say that.

“I am female. Does that make you uncomfortable?” she asked.

“Not at all. So, you have played this version of the game before?” Cameron asked, holding the game card out for her to see.

“Oh, yes. A long time ago. That’s the free game that everyone starts with,” she said without any condescension whatsoever. It made Cameron feel good not to be criticized for his level of gameplay. That was a real issue when he first started to get into gaming.

“So, I have the second clue figured out, but I went ahead and took a look at some of the others, and they have me stumped,” Cameron explained.

She looked at Cameron kind of sideways and asked, “Stumped? What is stumped?”

“Oh, I’m sorry. It means confused, I’m confused about what it means,” he explained. Cameron wasn’t sure, but he thought that he heard a familiar voice say, “Cam, you’re doing it,” as he interacted with Ebsar. He thought that was odd.

“So, now I know where you are in the game, but you will have to do the previous step to get the mixer before you will understand the step you are confused on for the combiner. I’m sorry,” said Ebsar. “I can introduce you to some of my friends to get you started, if you like?”

"That would be wonderful, thank you," said Cameron.

She took him by the hand and led him first to a locker where he could put the base that he was carrying around. Then, he spotted something he hadn't noticed before; there was a wide hallway just to the right of the arcade, around a corner that was also lined with shops and seating areas all along. It was along here that Ebsar introduced Cameron to the four different races of beings from whom he needed to gather the answers for the written questions.

"I am really glad that you want to help me with this. I have a few questions for you," said Cameron.

"It's my pleasure. I want to see you succeed at the game, even if it's the free one," Ebsar replied. "The next ones that you pay for get harder and harder as you progress, and if you don't get how the clues work, you will have to pay a little more along the way."

Cameron asked, "After I get the questions answered from the four races, how do I receive the next component?"

"Well, you have to get one of the question cards from the Prefect's window and fill it in. When you have them all filled in, you hand it to the Prefect, and he will give you the package with the mixer in it," Ebsar explained. "The components go together easily, and then you are off and ready for the next clue."

Cameron went back to the Prefect's window to get the question card and noticed that there were four sets, one for each race.

Catching up to Ebsar, Cameron arrived as she was talking with a being that had dull orange skin. He was tall and had a very expressive face. Cameron thought that his expressions were kind of over exaggerated, but he knew that he shouldn't judge something that he hadn't experienced before. As he thought this, he heard the soft, familiar voice again, "That's the way, Cam; good on you." Sonja was the only one that called him Cam, but how could it be her?

There were no other outstanding features on this being, other than slightly larger eyes and coarse hair on the backs of his arms. At least he was sure this time that he was male. Cameron waited to be introduced.

Ebsar began, "This is Dothax, and he is very happy to help. Dothax, this is my new friend, Cameron."

"Yes, Cameron, glad to meet you and to be helping you," Dothax offered. "I know the set of questions, and this might be very easy for you. I am thirty-five cycles and come from the Trellix realm. That makes me a Trellian, but since there are three races in the Trellix realm, I need to specify that I am Xala Trellian. There are also Mori Trellian and Layi Trellian." Dothax gave all of this information before giving Cameron a chance to say what he wanted from him. Cameron thought that this was an exercise in socialization with new races, but this guy didn't seem to be too interested in getting to know him; just in getting Cameron through the game, as if it were the most important thing. Cameron took note of this for future reference.

It was all he could do to keep up with writing down the answers, and half-expecting Dothax to lunge into another, he asked, "Why are you here?" but there was a pause. Cameron finished writing and began to ask when Dothax started in again.

"I come here quite often, and it's usually for the gaming and getting with acquaintances and associates although today there is a fresh shipment of ripe aspungents that I will buy and take back to Trellix and sell for a goodly, big profit," Dothax belted out in one breath. "That is, if I can keep myself from eating too many of them on the way."

As he finished writing, Cameron said, "I thank you for your time in answering the questions, and I hope that you can control yourself to a large profit with the aspungent things."

Dothax bowed away with, "My pleasure, I hope that you do well with the rest of the game."

"Well, Ebsar, who is next? That had absolutely no reference point in my brain, but very interesting in my imagination," said Cameron.

"I think that you don't get off of your world much, am I right?" Ebsar asked.

"Hardly ever, Ebsar," Cameron joked.

"I've communed a friend of mine that will meet us at the Jenu'Krull in a few nants. It's just up the hallway," Ebsar said.

Cameron asked, "What's a Jenu'Krull?"

"It's a place where the most dangerous games are begun. They are very advanced skill-level games, and some of them take many cycles to complete. Expensive they are, but the possible winnings are worth it to those willing to risk them," explained Ebsar.

"And your friend is good at these kinds of games?"

"Oh, yes. She is one of the best," she said.

This shocked Cameron because he would never have imagined that Ebsar was talking about a woman. He realized that it was a prejudiced way to think. They walked up the hallway where the kiosk stood for the Jenu'Krull games in front of a low walled arena that had benches along one side. There they sat waiting for Ebsar's friend.

Cameron thought of the time just then. How long had he been in the scenario and would Sonja ever show up? He worried about how much more he had to do and if he could finish it. Then he remembered that, regardless of how time ran in here, he would be back to reality between twenty-five and thirty-five minutes before he entered the venue. That was still hard for him to get his brain around.

A well-toned person approached wearing a uniform that showed off muscles and a strong form. It had a team emblem and what might be sponsors' logos affixed to it as well.

Cameron looked at her and said, "You must be Ebsar's friend. She told me about your competing in the Jenu'Krull games. Pleased to meet you; my name is Cameron Adams."

"Why must I be Ebsar's friend?" she shot back.

"Euthemia, I told Cameron that you were my friend. You are free to be whatever you want to be. Are we still friends?" asked Ebsar. "I bet on you often and tell others about you and the games."

"No worries, Ebsar, I am just messing with you. What can I do for you, Cameron?" asked Euthemia.

"Well, I am starting on the first game and would like you to answer the questions for the mixer," said Cameron.

She looked at him with a stern gaze and said, "Help me out, Ebsar. What were they? It's been so long ago."

Cameron spoke up, "The first I have. What is your name? If I have the correct spelling, we can go on to how old you are. E-u-t-h-e-m-i-a, is that correct?"

"That is right, and I am older than I look, but you need the number. I am thirty-three cycles of my home world, Gindyria," she said. "That only leaves the best question of all. Why am I here? You should tell him, Ebsar."

Ebsar looked startled as she turned to Euthemia and saw that she was serious, "Well, I don't know how much more famous you could get, but it is for fame that you are here."

Euthemia kind of struck a pose and said, "It's so much more meaningful coming from someone else and that way I'm not boasting."

"But you are kind of basking. Has it been an easy climb to your success?" asked Cameron.

"So, I train every day, and I have record kills in my division. At first it was hard, but now I just view it as coming to work at a skill that I have mastered," boasted Euthemia.

"These 'kills' are, of course, virtual, correct?" asked Cameron as he instantly realized the irony that he was, in fact, talking to a virtual character.

"Yes, but I always answer that with, 'would you want to tangle with me in reality?' and everybody just backs down," Euthemia answered. "So, you have what you need, and I have a game to get ready for. It was good talking with you, Cameron. See you around, Ebsar."

As Euthemia strolled back into the arena house, Cameron finished up his writing and sat down on one of the benches along the hallway.

"That's two down and two to go. You will have the mixer in no time, Cameron," said Ebsar. "As social interaction goes, I think that you should do the rest on your own. I might be giving you too much help and that could disqualify your end-game."

"Thank you for all your help so far. You can come with me for the other two, can't you?"

"I don't see why not, although I have to meet up with family in a little while. We are going to one of the restaurants here before I go back," explained Ebsar.

It suddenly occurred to Cameron that Ebsar could be the next race to get the answers from.

"Ebsar? That's your name. How old are you? I just realized that you could be one of the four. Where do you come from and why are you here?" Cameron rattled off. "I don't know why I didn't think of this before."

"Well, neither did I. Yes, that will help you immensely," said Ebsar. "Of course, my name is Ebsar, that's E-b-s-a-r, I am three-hundred seventy-eight encrants old, that is how time is measured on my home world of Zebrion."

"That's just wonderful, Ebsar. Thank you so much. Now why are you here?" asked Cameron and there was a long pause.

"I don't know quite how to say this," said Ebsar after a time. "Freedom is why. We need to be reminded what freedom is like I suppose. I miss it very much."

Cameron looked at how sad the thought made Ebsar look. "I don't understand. Aren't you free? You just told me that you were going to have a meal with your family before you go home."

"I didn't say I was going home, I just said before I go. I am a prisoner let out for an occasional excursion so that we, my kind, don't go crazy and do things that would be disastrous in our holdings," explained Ebsar. "I know that to look at me, I'm not much, but if one from my race is confined for too long there can be an actual explosion that could take out about one hundred square meters."

"But what is your crime?" asked Cameron. "I haven't seen anyone guarding you."

"My crime is that I am Zebrin. We are closely monitored with very sophisticated nanotechnology that reads our level of frustration and anxiety. If it gets to a certain point, we are taken out, either physically or by dissolution," Ebsar explained. "We should be glad and thankful for the nice planet that was provided for us, though; it keeps us away from the masses for their safety."

Cameron didn't even want to know what dissolution meant but had to stop and think if something like this situation applied to anything from the history of Earth. Putting people away from the human population because they are a threat to society, yes, but rehabilitation programs are usually in place for criminals and mental patients. The only thing that came to Cameron's mind were penal colonies.

"No matter how bizarre these scenarios get, I can be sure that there is some takeaway for reality," said Cameron out loud.

"What do you mean, Cameron?" asked a perplexed Ebsar.

"Oh, nothing, just thinking out loud," said Cameron. "I can hardly believe that an entire planet is a prison complex."

"It's easier if you know that the landmass is one very small island surrounded by high salt content ocean water," said Ebsar. "Compared to most worlds, it's barely livable. There are other, much smaller islands that we can fly to from time to time for a change of scenery, but most of the time we live on the Grandland, as they call it."

'That must be terrible for their race. I wish that I could do something about it,' thought Cameron.

"I am not even sure that any solution that I could come up with would have as broad of an effect as it would need to have. Just know this, that where you have met me and cared for me and my needs in my journey, you are able to do in the lives of so many in need back on Zebrion. You are an effective, caring person, and I thank you for that. People place themselves in prisons and hide away from others for whom they should be concerned. You have that concern for others, Ebsar."

Just then, Cameron thought he heard a reassuring cooing from Sonja in the back of his mind. He looked down at Ebsar and noticed her getting all teary-eyed. He hid that he saw it by saying, "So now I need one more, and I can get the mixer. I suppose I have to do that on my own, right? So here I go, wish me luck."

Cameron went out into the crowd of beings, searching for the next interview and thinking that being busy would make him less vulnerable to the emotions he stirred in Ebsar, but mostly in himself. Walking further down the hall, he noticed a person sitting on one of the benches along a stretch of shops that had a common design motif of what Cameron would consider frilly and feminine. The young man was hunched over a brochure as if studying it for a test. He had distinct features that were very bold. A strong, chiseled face with deep-set eyes and a square jaw that made him seem rather stern. Cameron, knowing that he couldn't judge a person by their looks, as a book by its cover, introduced himself.

"Hi, my name is Cameron Adams," he announced. "Are you here for the games?"

Turning slowly toward Cameron, he said, "No, I don't usually get into them anymore. I'm looking for a friend that I can take back to Nilonerth for life mating."

"Well, I'm not from around here, as you can no doubt tell. Is that like what my race calls marriage, if you have ever heard of it, that is?" asked Cameron. "I just would like to have you answer the questions on the game card for the first free game, but it would be great to try and understand a little about where you come from as well."

"Oh, I remember that. Sure, no problem. My name is Itera Coliany, I'm seventy encrants and, like I have already mentioned, from Nilonerth," Itera offered. "The purpose of my journey is two-fold. I have to buy seed for my farm, and I would like to find a life mate."

"Wow, that's the same measure of time my new friend uses on her planet, Zebrion. Is that a coincidence or what?" mused Cameron. "Do you know of her planet?"

"I most certainly do. Could you introduce me to her?" Itera asked. "I've given you all that you need to fill in the answers, and I would consider it a fine gesture to have you introduce me to her. These places here on this portion of the mall are practically useless for getting in touch with females."

"Well, I can do that, but do you know that she is a prisoner?" asked Cameron. "And do you know why she is a prisoner?"

"I would wager that everyone here knows about the plight of the Zebrin, and if she will have me, we will become life mates, and she will be free from her incarceration once and for all as long as she stays with me on my home world. That is the law," explained Itera. "So now, Cameron Adams of earth, will you introduce me to her?"

Shocked at the response, Cameron said, "Yes, yes, let me go and get her."

"I will come along," Itera sang happily after him.

Feeling quite accomplished after his matchmaking, Cameron turned in the game card with the completed answers from the four people he interviewed and was given the mixer. It was about the same size as the base but only four inches high with four compartments in it. The material seemed to be clear plexiglass with tapered bottoms that all slanted toward the outside corners; there were holes there that looked as though they would accept some sort of attachment from underneath. He was turning to leave the ticket booth at the Prefect's storefront when he heard, "Ae, wait, yurfurgot the bottles." He turned back to see a small box being handed to him with four bottles of clear liquid in them. They were numbered one through four corresponding with the four compartments in the mixer.

Looking more closely at the mixer, Cameron noticed that, hovering over each of the holes, there were small propellers that didn't seem to be attached to anything. He wasn't sure why or how they could work, as any kind of device to mix the fluids but being assured by Ebsar that it would work, he put it with the base in his locker.

The clue for the combiner made more sense now, but the tubes were the next item on the list and for that, there was a clue and a task. 'Four become one and reflect well on you,' is what it said about the tubes. As Cameron began puzzling over the clue, he tried to take it logically and literally. There had been four persons that he interviewed for the mixer, and he received the elixirs as well. There was no clue for the elixirs by themselves, but the task to accomplish in order to get the tubes was hard enough. He was hoping that it would come packaged with the mixer, but no such luck. The task read, 'Discover the four stories' reflections,' and under that, 'Find in the mall something from your past that was very meaningful and buy it. Explaining that to the shop owner, you will have completed the task.'

As he sat puzzling further, Dothax and Euthemia came strolling by, arm in arm. He could hardly believe his eyes. Had they gotten together on account of him? This could be what it meant by reflecting well on him. First Itera and Ebsar, and now Dothax and Euthemia; that's four becoming one, well, two and two, but still. Then, he thought that it must be a coincidence and that the clue had to mean 'four becoming one,' not two sets of two becoming two sets of one. Besides, it's an Earth-saying about marriage after all, and this was definitely not Earth.

As he thought more about how he could combine these four beings into one, he got to thinking that the things each one wanted and the reasons that each was here at the mall had essentially been acquired. Ebsar was here for companionship, and it became love and freedom; Itera was after the same thing—love—and it would grant Ebsar freedom, something she thought would never happen to her. Cameron wasn't sure if Dothax would get wealthy from his sale of aspungents, but if what he saw by way of a new relationship being formed with Euthemia, her fame would bring him wealth, as well. Cameron could say that, all in all, the four situations did reflect well on him. But to turn it into something tangible in order to hand it over for the tubes? He wasn't sure that he had figured anything out for certain other than that he felt very accomplished for a day's work. Was this just a game?

Cameron was lost and confused without Ebsar to help him, so he wandered back to the Prefect's storefront to beg for a clue as to how to accomplish the first part of the task for the tubes. When he got there, the Prefect asked him to tell the stories, so Cameron proceeded to tell him the same things that he was trying to glean from the four encounters with the beings that he interviewed. When he was done, he said, "If there is something that I should have gleaned from this step that I wasn't able to, I give up and will count myself to have failed the game. I can leave now." He started to hold his breath in anticipation.

"No, yer didz good and fin. Now yer needs ta go to the store," the Prefect said as he pointed down the hallway.

Cameron felt better that he was on the right track and so headed down the hall. It was a hall that he hadn't been down before, and the shops were starting to look halfway normal. He came to an Earth-type sporting shop and went in without hesitation. There was sporting equipment from every sport he could imagine, but one item in the whole store drew his complete attention. It was a baseball glove. It was just like the one that his dad had bought for him when he was five years old. There was a poster that came with the one he had gotten from his dad that was still hanging on his bedroom wall. This one didn't have that, but he noticed the price was in herns—18.00 herns. What was he going to do? What was a hern? As he put his hands in his pockets, he discovered a paper bill that he took out. It was a 20.00 hern note. How it got there he couldn't say, but Sonja's holalectrum was not in his pocket anymore, which had him worried.

He went up with the glove and paid for it, telling the store owner that it had sentimental value, and, true to the Prefect's word, the owner handed over a box with the tubes in it. Cameron was as excited as he would be on Christmas morning and yet, remembering that the mixer came with the bottles, waited for anything else that may come with it. "Nope, that be all fur ya," was the response from the owner.

There was, however, a clue in the box for the next item, the top seat. On the way to his locker, he took the note out and looked it over. It read, 'Who must occupy the top seat in your life?' As he was on Cameron's mind, he thought instantly of his dad only he was not quite sure if it was his real dad or just a recurring dream that he used to have.

As he continued on to his locker, he looked up to see a man coming towards him. He got the impression that it was his dad, but that couldn't be, could it? The man held out a holalectrum that shone with the color carmine red which was his dad's name. How he knew that it was specifically carmine red and not just plain old red, he couldn't say; it was just a feeling. As soon as he gathered the image and held it in his mind, it faded into nothing, and the glove vanished as well. There was a great sadness that came over Cameron as if his past had faded away with the glove, along with the image of his dad.

Cameron thought deeply and came up with the idea that the past is the past, and the lessons of the past can be learned and viewed with a new perspective; he was forging his own future. He himself should be the top seat of his life. The holalectrum that he has to put in the top seat must be gamboge, not Sonja's green or his dad's carmine red. He wiped tears away from his eyes, and they became clear enough to see that the top seat was included in the box with the tubes; or perhaps he just noticed it there, but he was sure that it was not there just a moment ago. Things were getting stranger every minute in this place, and he wished it were over. Now to find out where to get his own holalectrum.

Finally reaching the locker alcove, Cameron placed the tubes and top seat in and noticed a vending machine that dispensed bags to carry purchases in. How ironic that the price was two herns per bag, just what he had left. He bought one and put it in his locker with the parts.

With all of the running around getting information and items for the game, Cameron hadn't noticed that this was a mall after all. He started seeing storefronts and shops, kiosks and food counters along the hallways. Names for these places were quite different from what Cameron was used to in the real world, and they were filled with goods and items that he had never seen before either. One such place was called Spectraderm, and as Cameron sat for a bit and watched, people of various races would go in with one color skin and come out multicolored or with colors that would move or change with the way the light reflected off it. Some of them would have colors that would dance and morph into pictures or other colors.

He also noticed that gaming was a large part of the mall complex and that there were symbols that corresponded to the various game franchises that were offered for play. The name signs had the symbols listed for the different games along with whatever they were selling. A shoe store would sell footwear that enhanced gameplay for certain games listed by its symbol or clothing to match an era of the fantastic styles and environments of the games.

One shop that caught Cameron's eye was called 'Step Up, Set Up Sites' because it had the logo for the game he was playing. There were many other symbols listed on the sign, but he was on the first free game, and there was a special deal. 'First game free sites,' it said, and it reminded Cameron of the small print on the game card he was given that said the contraption had to be assembled in a quiet, solitary place without distractions. It crossed his mind that Trelic Blue most likely hadn't taken advantage of this offer since he could walk to the place where he assembled his first device. Cameron thought that he would try one, since it was a free offer to players of the first free game.

Cameron went into the shop where the banner over the door read 'Step into Solitude.' There were large posters of exotic, faraway places to go.

"How do I get to these places if I were to choose one?"

Cameron asked a very thin, blue-skinned humanoid that stood behind a counter. He wasn't thin like skinny, but thin like narrow from the sides inward. His face was on the front of a head smooshed together from both sides. It was fine once you got used to seeing him; he actually had pleasant features. "I see that some are not offered with the free game, but this one at the top of a snow-covered mountain would be great."

"So, that one is with the special offer, but it is very unpredictable with the weather and such. It's situated high up where the air is thin, like me. The vault is in the back of the store there." He pointed as he came out from behind the counter with four legs. He scurried along with Cameron to what were labeled 'Virtual Portways.' "You will have to bring your components with you, though. Once you enter with a code that I will give you, there is a lock so others can't invade your space and take your parts."

"Can I see how it works?" asked Cameron, as he started for one of the vaults.

"Sure, just give me the number from your game card, and I will get you a code," said the proprietor.

Cameron called out the number from memory. "1138," he said. And with that, the man went to enter the numbers into his machine on the counter. Out popped an orange-colored card that he brought over to the vault entrance where Cameron was standing. After inserting the card in a slot next to the door, it opened onto a scene that took both of their breaths away. As they both stepped through the threshold, the vault door closed, and the only thing that was left visible from the inside facing the door was the card slot on a white pole. The air was relatively calm but freezing cold, and the view was spectacular to the point of almost being indescribable. First, there was a ridge that was wide enough to safely walk out on to a flat, level spot that was raised slightly, as if it were made especially for assembling the contraptions for the games. Over each side were steep, slightly angled slopes downward into deep valleys that seemed to never end at a bottom but rather to fade into hazy darkness. The view to the horizon was a 360-degree feast for the eyes with mountain peaks stretching off into the distance in every direction. The time of day with the sunlight blazing made everything stunningly sharp and crisp as if it had been captured as a still image and set into crystal.

"This is perfect," said Cameron, shivering. "With the sun so sharp and bright, I don't think that I will use a coat or jacket at all for the short time that I will be in here."

"Suit yourself, but I told you that it's unpredictable,"
the man said.

"I will bring what I have so far and the only other item that I still need is the holalectrum. Could you tell me where I can get one?" Cameron asked. "I had one with me almost this whole time, but it vanished. I was on the search for someone or someplace to get my own when I found your store," he added as he inserted the card into the slot for the vault door. It opened onto the drab, little shop, and Cameron darted off to retrieve the contraption from the locker he had put the pieces in without waiting for an answer from the proprietor.

On the way back from getting the components to his contraption, Cameron went what he thought was a shortcut to get back to the 'Step Up, Set Up Sites' shop. As he turned one corner, he thought that he was totally lost when he came to a kiosk that had gems for sale. He looked them over and found one that was his color, gamboge, but he didn't have any money to pay for it. He was a bit wary of the place as they weren't calling the gems *holalectrum*, but simply gemstones. "Do you have any holalectrum?" he asked, and the whole kiosk swished away in a cloud of sooty mist. Looking down, Cameron noticed a single gamboge colored holalectrum.

Very stunned, Cameron picked up the gem and continued on his way to the shop walking in a daze. Cameron thought that he heard his name being called in the distance, so he turned his ear to the direction of Guum Square. Sure enough, he heard it. His package had arrived. He took off running since he still had no idea how long a nant was.

The loudspeaker sang out: "Cameron Gamboge, your package has arrived in compartment theta twelve. You have twenty-eight nantz to pick it up. Cameron Gamboge, your package has arrived in compartment theta twelve. You have twenty-eight nantz to pick it up."

At least he had more time than Trelic had. As he ran to the place where all the compartments were and found the one with the thetas marked on them, a thought crossed his mind—I wonder what happens to the packages that don't get picked up? Counting down from the higher numbers, (there were twenty-four), he got to the twelfth one. It was a cube wrapped in shiny, orange cloth, just like Trelic's blue package. Cramming the box into his bag, Cameron ran to find the shop he was bound for before he heard his name being called. It was all a blur, but he suddenly found himself in front of the 'Step Up, Set Up Sites' shop in no time. Realizing that this was almost it, he rushed in and over to the vault where he had his code stored. He quickly entered 1138 on the keypad, and the door opened to a dark, stormy blizzard. This was very unexpected, but the proprietor warned him that it was unpredictable. He wasn't sure if he could assemble the contraption in such conditions, but he would try. He struggled to the platform, brought the base out and set it on the raised dais. Next, the mixer could be attached in its four corners with the compartments numbered one to the top left, two to the right, three in the bottom right corner and four to the left of that. The bottles he un-capped one at a time and poured in each corresponding numbered compartment, and the tiny propellers began to spin, mixing the four clear liquids into their true colors. Number one was gold, two was orange, three was blue and four was pink.

The tubes were next, and they went on without spilling a drop of the liquid from the compartments, even though the wind was raging, and the spitting snow was mixed with hail and Cameron could hardly steady his frozen fingers. The tubes had the attachment for the top seat to fasten into and just above where the holalectrum was to be seated, there was a place for the lens to be inserted.

The combiner fastened over the mixer between the place

where the top seat and lens holder were situated, and as soon as he snapped it into place, the four colors combined to mix into, of all colors, carmine red. Cameron knew, without being good in art class, that those four colors could not mix and combine to make any shade of red. The gamboge holalectrum settled into its saddle, and the last piece, the lens, was ready to be inserted.

As Cameron stretched to put the lens in place, the snow blinding him and the cold stinging his very mind, the beam of light shot upward into the night sky, illuminating the blizzard activity swirling around it. A narrow beam of gamboge laser light shot straight up, creating a tunnel through the clouds and stretching far into space. The defining applause sounded, and a giant number was projected in laser lights piercing the stormy night sky: 28%

The scene shimmered and shifted to open up into a bright, white light, and Cameron found himself standing at a game console in the arcade of the Eastfield mall, ready to drop a token in the slot that he was looking for. He was a little disoriented, and the game in front of him was not Alpha Generate, the one he had been standing in front of when he went into the scenario, but Joust, a game he loathed and would never play. He backed away from it and returned the token to his pocket. There it was, the holalectrum gem that he found from the food court.

As he thought about his performance in the 'game,' he was proud of the score he received and walked across the hall to sit and rest on one of the benches. After a few minutes he started to get hungry and wished that Sonja would come back so they could find something more to eat.

Just then, Sonja did come running down the hall and noticed Cameron sitting on the bench across from the arcade.

“I was in a frantic fit when I noticed that my holalectrum was missing. I got here as fast as I could, but I was unable to enter the gate at the same time signature that you were at,” Sonja said, panting frantically. “There has to be synchronicity between all of the entities that enter the gate. The time that a group enters achieves this if they all enter within a few minutes of each other. If there is too much time lag between them, the synchronicity is lost and so is the possibility of catching up to them if you enter late.”

“I had the key. You knew what would happen with this scenario, right? And you taught me how to exit correctly, so don’t get all excited,” Cameron said as he noticed that Sonja had on a new pair of shoes. “I think that I did all right on my own and you couldn’t have been too worried if you took time to go get new shoes. My download was 28%, that’s three over the minimum, so what do you think of that?”

“Well, technically the score can never go above the 20% mark so you must have done something to cheat it,” said Sonja.

“Oh, you mean like the Kobayashi Maru test in Star Trek, right?” Cameron shot back.

“I have no idea what that is,” she said as they headed for the exit of the mall.

On the drive home, Cameron told Sonja the whole story of what happened in the venue; what the scenario was and what he thought he learned from it.

"I am always amazed and awed by the many creatures that are found in these venues and wish that I could play them as VR games with my friends," said Cameron. "My hat is off to the team that came up with the graphics and software for this one especially."

"You know, I was with you in parts, don't you?"

"Yes, there were times that I knew that I heard you and your approval. That really helped me along. How did you do that without your holalectrum?"

"I want you to know, Cam, that I'm happy with your progress," she said, ignoring him. "This last gate took you to places that showed you how concern and compassion for others is vitally important in the work that is ahead for the human race. But now, you need some rest. We shouldn't get back too late, and you should go right to bed. Tomorrow, I will let you sleep in and we can just go to a park and relax. I do want to go over what you experienced from today's scenario though, but for the most part, it will be a relaxing day."

When Sonja dropped Cameron off at his house, he got out and waved goodbye to her, thrusting his other hand into his pocket.

There, to his utter amazement, he found that he had the real gamboge holalectrum that he had found in the venue.

Chapter Six:

The Park

The next morning was Sunday and true to Sonja's word, Cameron was able to sleep until nine o'clock. He got up, and Chuck had already taken Sandy out for her walk and was away with his friends. His mom and dad were at church, no doubt. Sometimes he would go with them, but he was sure that they knew how late he had gotten in and just let him sleep. He made a leisurely breakfast and sat back on the couch to be still and ponder what his life had become. It had only been a month since he met Sonja, yet it felt like a lot longer. 'What could she be getting me ready to do or be?' he thought. 'Why would I need the gamboge holalectrum from the mall scenario? Would I be opening light gates with it? And for what purpose?'

In the midst of these questions, Sonja pulled up in front of his house and came to the door.

“I don’t want any today, Sonja. I’m resting, it’s the day of rest,” Cameron said as he let her in.

“Oh, I’m not here to take you on any great adventure today, just to a park to relax and talk,” she said rather nonchalantly. “We can talk about yesterday’s scenario. I’m sorry that I wasn’t able to be there with you. Where did you get my holalectrum by the way? I forgot to ask
you last night.”

As they were getting into the car, he explained the events up to the time that he started to play the Alpha Generate game.

“That’s when I realized that the gem was how you opened the light gates, but this time it was different,” he said. “I was kind of drawn into the game; I didn’t see the ribbon of light open, just a blazing white light that faded into the venue.”

“Some gates are different. We’ve been doing this for a long time and technology changes.”

“There you go with the ‘we’ stuff again. How long before you can tell me just what is up with this whole thing?”

“Actually, it won’t be long now, but today is for relaxing and talking, with just one short venue,” she said, without Cameron even noticing it.

After cruising for some time, Cameron said, "You know, there are parks in town we could have gone to instead of driving all the way out here."

"Then we wouldn't have had the peace and quiet of being out among nature. You do like getting away from it all once in a while, don't you, Cam?" Sonja asked with a smirk. "At least to the wilderness of the computer screen, right? I'm talking about real peace and quiet where you can just rest and relax. Besides, it's only two miles from town."

"Well, what about all those birds and rustling sounds? Not so peaceful after all," said Cameron.

"Uh, that would be the wind blowing through the trees, and news flash, bird sounds are peaceful. Close your eyes and just listen. These natural sounds are what your ears and brain have been missing," said Sonja. "Just think of this place as being carved out away from all the busyness of the city, or in this case, town and school and friends and every care and concern—for the purpose of relaxing."

"Some people find relaxation in work or sports or in the games they play," said Cameron.

"Here you can bring your own recreation or food or music, but it is intended for peacefully enjoying the natural environment around you. To rest. It's free, paid for by your tax dollars. There is a duck pond that you can fish in, a playground for the kids, trees and walking paths and benches for just sitting," said Sonja. "What is wrong with that?"

They pulled into the park and didn't find any other cars or bikes in the parking area.

"Okay, you have me here. Now, we need to talk about yesterday's scenario," said Cameron.

Sonja got out and went to open the trunk of her car. She grabbed out a basket and a blanket.

"Not so fast, Cam, we came here to relax, first and foremost. We have a long time to consider yesterday," she returned. "I want us to do something first."

That had Cameron a little nervous, especially when she said, "Let's put this blanket down over here under these trees and lie down together."

Cameron just looked at her, and she continued, "Get your mind out of the gutter. We are just going to lie here, close our eyes, listen and rest. Nothing more."

As they lay there, just being quiet, Sonja said, "First, we need to just listen to the sounds all around us, breathe deeply and relax with our eyes closed. The birds, the wind in the trees and in the tall grass, the water in the background in the little brook that feeds into the pond. Listen and relax for a moment."

This went on for what Cameron thought was a long time, but

actually, it was only ten minutes.

"Now," Sonja went on, "think about what you took or learned from yesterday's scenario."

"The contraption was a genius insert, the way it came together and what the significance of each piece was. I was impressed."

"That was all just internal stuff," said Sonja. "The real work was the individual interviews and getting to know people. Finding out what their needs were and affecting change in their lives, that was the real work. You might have learned some things about yourself and where you come from, but it was just to carry you along to the real work. All this against the backdrop of community."

They were still for a while longer, just listening and resting until Sonja continued, "Do you remember the center that we stopped at just before the mall? Now that was the prime example of a community stepping up to meet the needs of the people."

"You know, now that you mention it, there was a sense of community in the scenario even though the people, or beings, were from all over the universe. There was a group identity achieved among them," Cameron said. "I felt like I fit in although I knew that it wasn't real and that I was just another character in the elaborate drama of the quest. I guess that's how it must be like to get out into the real world; you meet new people and visit strange, different cultures. I suppose that the real-world takeaway is knowing how to face real situations, as if

I had something in common with others and something worthwhile to offer those whom I try to work with and help."

"So, you think that you can help them?" said Sonja. "That's proof to me that you have made progress."

"But help who? What is this all about?" Cameron questioned. "Do you remember when you started to use 'we' in our conversations and said that you would tell me about it eventually? The 'we' you always start to mention and make up an excuse for? The first time you said, 'We know that learning is made easier when all of our senses are engaged.' And when I questioned it, you said that it was just a slip."

"That was a long time ago, Cam. How did you remember that?"

"It was just after we finished at the zoo, after I got sick. And you quickly changed the subject," replied Cameron. "Then, another time when we were going to go to the mall you said, 'We have a lesson today that I think you will love.'"

"I'm impressed," she said rather shocked. "This shows me your keen sense for details and a good memory."

"Would you stop doing that, as if you are always evaluating me for some job position? And just now your words were, 'Some gates are different. We have been doing this for a long time and technology changes.' Who are the 'we' already?"

"Please, Cam, I will tell you everything soon. Let's continue the day and see where it takes us," she pleaded.

Cameron looked disgusted and turned away. They both just lay there with their eyes closed. Cameron started thinking and going over in his mind all the events that led up to this point when he heard voices getting closer and closer.

Kevin and Bill came riding up on their bikes. They each had fishing poles and tackle boxes with them. For some strange reason, Cameron was nervous when he saw them coming.

"I hope you don't mind. I invited Kevin, Bill and Peter to come along, but I don't see Peter," said Sonja. "I have a short scenario I would like to include them in, if it's alright with you. I really want them to be in the game when we play baseball, but I need to know if they will be able to handle it. There are no difficult quests or tasks to accomplish in it, just a sample or demo of what the environment is like."

"Well, I haven't had many times with you where we haven't gone into one of your light gates, so, what was I thinking? Of course, it's all right with me," Cameron sarcastically answered. "Why did you invite Peter? I thought he was learning another way."

"No, Cam, he is excelling rapidly with the VR, and in other ways. I just wanted you and your friends to meet him and allow him to be included in the game we plan to have. I'm allowing Bill and Kevin to have a glimpse of the training so that when you are through, they have some understanding of what you went through," she explained. "In the coming days, teamwork is going to be a vital tool in holding it all together for the human race, and we try to include the friends and relatives as much as we can get away with."

"Why haven't you told my parents or brother about it?"

"Let's pick up on that some other time, Cam. Your friends are coming now," she said. "Hi, guys. I see that you brought your fishing gear along. Did you meet up with Peter along the way?"

They came up all out of breath, and Bill said, "Man, this is a long way out on a bike. We saw him coming up behind us, but he's slow."

"We heard that there was good fishing here. Did anyone bring something to eat?" asked Kevin.

They sat down at one of the tables near the small lake, and Sonja got some snacks from her basket. They munched, talked and waited for Peter to show up. Cameron asked to use Bill's fishing pole, and he and Kevin went to the water to throw in their lines. It was a laid-back day.

Peter came along just as Kevin and Cameron were pulling their third fish from the lake. They had a five-gallon pail of water to put them in, but most likely they would let them go before they left the park.

Sonja called everyone to come around the table and began to explain a few things. "Glad you could make it, Peter. We can load the bikes on the car when we're done here today. This is supposed to be just a rest day for Peter and Cameron. But I thought that it was about time that you, Bill and Kevin, were let in on some of what is going on."

"Well, Bill and I would like to know why you're seeing Peter. Aren't you and Cameron kind of dating or together somehow?" asked Kevin. "I mean, besides the adventures that you go on in some kind of new virtual reality game system, what's up?"

"We're just friends, Kevin," she said.

"You and Peter, or you and Cameron?" Kevin shot back.

"Why this questioning? They're both my friends, and that's pretty much where it's at," she said with finality. "I would like for you and Bill to be my friends, too. That's why I have planned to show you what the light gates are all about. They are a training tool, but they can be a lot of fun, as well. I'm sure Cameron has told you about the virtual worlds that he has experienced. I'm sure that you will have a great time, especially all of you together in something that we have put together for a demo."

Bill spoke up and asked, "Is this some kind of Beta test that we are going to be part of as testers for a new game system?"

"No, but I wish it were only that. There are very serious reasons for the use of such technology. I will tell you more when you come out," Sonja said as she walked over to a large tree by the lake. Right beside the tree there began a strip of light that started up about seven feet and zipped down to the ground; it was glowing with white light shimmering like lightning. The intensity of the light showed that the strip was opening from the bottom to the top, and Sonja told them that they could go in whenever they were ready.

“Can I be frank with all of you? Don’t tell anybody what you are about to experience. The fate of the world may lay in the balance. I know that you might think that that is silly sounding, but it may be truer than any of you have ever imagined,” Sonja said with a slightly sinister tone. Cameron thought that she was setting them up for the virtual reality scenario that she had planned for them, but he also knew that there was something to her words. He didn’t like the possible truth that they conveyed.

Peter was the first to scamper through, and the rest followed. Cameron glanced over to see Sonja standing back. “You’re not coming in?”, he asked.

“No, not this time. It won’t be long. We’ll talk more afterwards,” she said as she took a seat to wait for their return.

As the group stepped through the gate, they instantly felt the motion of the starship they boarded. The main view of space showed an extremely high rate of speed, more than could be possible. The stars were short distortions of light, and the planets would come into view just long enough for them to identify that they were touring through the solar system of earth.

The room that they were in was some kind of bridge not too dissimilar to the Enterprise from Star Trek, but different enough to have its own source and character. The planets of their solar system were being passed as if they were in ordered alignment with each other. They knew that that couldn't be true, but it didn't much matter for the thrill of the ride. They came up on Mars, and it wasn't long before Earth was in view. Next Venus and Mercury went zooming past—and they were headed straight for the Sun.

As soon as they passed Mercury, the ship began to accelerate to an unimaginable rate until the Sun completely filled the view screen. Everything turned bright white and bleached out to nothingness. There was a high-pitched sound that threatened to rise to an ear-splitting crescendo until it suddenly stopped, and everything was blackness and void.

It wasn't like the blackness of space because there were no stars. There was nothing for the four of them to focus on at all. Then, slowly the light began to dawn as the sun rose over a futuristic skyline of a city that looked like it was designed for a comic book illustration. The four found that they were now in a flying car which flew to meet the rising light over the city. They were swooping and darting throughout the many tall buildings and walk bridges and transparent transport tubes that ran pneumatic cylinders; the sensation was like being on a roller coaster.

There was a roller coaster as well that ran winding through the city with high, steep climbs and deadfalls with loops and corkscrews and long, angled curves extending out over the bay. There was a plunge into the water for which they could not see an exit.

"I have *got* to try that. Where can we get on it?" Bill excitedly asked. Suddenly, as if the flying car heard him, it changed course in a long arc to the left at an incredible angle, swooped down to one of the large buildings and finally came to a stop on one of the many landings high over the street level.

As they climbed out of the car, each one in turn noticed that each other had changed into avatars like in a video game. There was enough realism to enable them to recognize each other but just enough difference to creep them out if they looked at one another long enough. "This is weird," said Kevin. And all of them had to agree with him. "Our skin texture is like leather to look at, but it feels as soft as silk."

On their way to get on the roller coaster, they looked out over the city. There was so much crisp, new architecture and the city itself was sparkling clean. As they paused to take it all in, suddenly, there was a flash that changed everything into a dull, filthy gray slum of a place with a thick haze-like fog settling into every crevice. The buildings looked as if they had endured a war. It was just for a brief instant and then lightning flashed and it was back to the modern, futuristic splendor, glittering in the bright sunlight once again.

"All right, did you guys just see that? Like the city turned gray and old?" asked Cameron.

"Yes, I did," replied Kevin. "Like a glitch in the matrix. What do you suppose it could mean?"

Peter spoke up and said, "It could be just that. A flaw that kind of bled through the software of the scenario. There must be several layers of construct underneath these things."

"Or it could be like the older version of the game we were playing a while back that had old servers pointing to different versions of the game," said Bill. "Remember the one where we all started out together in the beginning? As soon as we went on the dungeon quests, it made no sense when some of us found ourselves playing through outdated levels, thinking they counted toward the main objective."

"It makes you wonder if these scenarios are on servers somewhere or just some brand-new technology that we couldn't begin to fathom," said Cameron. "Anyway, let's take a roller coaster ride."

Walking over to the entrance of the roller coaster, they fell into a short queue of local people that were going on as well. There was no cost which surprised them, although in a virtual reality prepared especially for them, they would have had the money or whatever type of currency was required for the things they were able to do.

As they stepped into the roller coaster car and sat down, it was as easy to pull the bar to their laps. That action started the car moving. Advancing ahead about 300 feet, they could see the city laid out in a grid of deep canyons and high building peaks with the roller coaster tracks strewn throughout the city like spaghetti. At the edge of the landing, the first deadfall was almost straight down. There was an abrupt bank to the right and then a corkscrew which ended in a long, vertical climb. They thought it would never end.

Finally, they crested a very tall skyscraper where the track arched over into a mind-shatteringly steep descent straight down into the darkness of the ground level of the city. The track leveled off and followed a grid just above the streets with sharp banking turns at each intersection. Then it was up again and down again until they came to the bay area. There was a very long gradual rise out over the water of the bay. The coaster car was incredibly high up over the water as it crested and came straight down to plunge into the bay.

With water all around them, they discovered that the car and track was in a tube and continued to do loops and high-banking corkscrews with high climbs and low falls, all before coming to a stop at a kind of underwater transportation hub. They could stay seated and continue on with the roller coaster or get off and take either the pneumatic transport tube or a small gauge train ride that wandered off into a large cave.

“What do you think, guys?” asked Cameron. “The pneumatic tube would surely take us back to the city like a subway, as will the roller coaster, but the train looks like it is going to take us into the dungeon like in our favorite game."

"Not a hard choice, Cameron," said Bill. "Lead the way."

Peter and Kevin agreed, and they were all out of their seats and walking toward the train. As it chugged and clanked away, they noticed a light glowing up ahead with the noise of pikes and shovels working away striking rock. As they drew closer into what looked like a vast community of workers with campfires and small huts built up in a kind of makeshift village, they got a glimpse of the ore they were mining. It looked like multicolored crystals all clumped together with bulbous salt-like growths holding them together.

Stepping off the train, they were all handed tools, sleeping bags and a box that appeared to have some supplies in it: first aid items, some food, and a flashlight, among other things.

Peter took what he was handed and asked the man that gave the supplies out, "What's the ore that is being mined?"

The man said, "What are you, a wise guy? It's holalectrum, of course," as if everyone should know that.

"Hold on a minute," exclaimed Cameron. "That's what the holalectrum are made from. Are you kidding me? What is the significance of this crystal?"

As the man overheard Cameron's comments, he offered this explanation. "You four are, no doubt, not workers sent from the surface. Am I right?"

"You couldn't be more right about that, sir," said Kevin.

"Well, then, judging by your clothing and the lost looks on your faces, I will fill you in on what this is all about. We don't get much advertising for what has to be done down here," the man said. "This mineral, holalecium, was discovered after the war to have near miraculous healing and technological properties that have turned the world right side up again after such devastation."

"Guys, that must be what we caught a glimpse of off the landing earlier," said Bill.

As if that realization had anything to do with it, the whole scene changed. The tools that they had been given turned into weapons like the ones they would have chosen in one of their favorite RPG dungeon crawler games. Now, instead of picking and digging for the ore, they had to fight their way through the level to obtain as much of it as they could. It was great fun, just like a Saturday night, and, boy, did they rack up
a pile of ore.

The fighting continued until they came to a boss in the middle of a dais surrounded by bubbling water that shot up orange and green flames now and then. They arranged themselves just like in one of their multiplayer games to take down the beast: range fighter, healer, tank and berserker. As the dragon-like monster surged his last, the scenario began to fade as the score came flashing in the air: to everyone's amazement, they received a combined total of 83%.

When they came back through the light gate, Bill was first, quickly followed by Peter, Kevin and after a little while, Cameron. Sonja was sitting there ready to greet them.

"How was it, guys?" she asked.

"That was so cool! The most fun I've *ever* had with a virtual experience in my life," said Bill. "How does it work? I want one, but what is it? All we know is that a light ribbon opens up by some means, and the insides are bigger than the outsides, like the Tardis in Dr. Who, only on a world scale." He was rambling with excitement.

"Yah, and no marks on my face from any headset," Kevin added. "You were right, Cameron, there's no way to figure this thing out."

There was nothing to give them the indication of time dilation as the reference points were not crucial for their proximity to the events both inside and outside the gate. Their position didn't have anything to do with the shifting time.

"I'm sorry, boys," said Sonja, "but the technology is not available in stores. It is for training purposes only, and the details are top secret. I am not working for the military, mind you, just an organization that is very much concerned for the survival and perpetuation of the human race. Like I said before you went into the gate, don't tell anybody."

Sonja doubted whether she should have revealed the light gates to them, but it was essential to have them on board with Cameron's assignments for his future. If the plan was to work, it needed close companions that could work well together.

They got the three bikes strapped to the back of Sonja's car somehow, and she drove Cameron, Kevin, Bill and Peter into town. The conversation in the car was as excited as if they had just been picked up from the greatest summer camp of their lives. Even Peter, who was kind of shy and stand-offish, was talking a mile a minute. Cameron thought to himself how good life was with such friends; if what Sonja had been telling him about the survival of the human race were true, he could see that purpose would require such good, close friends.

Sonja dropped Cameron off at his house, telling him that it was a good day and that the test went well. "And don't you feel rested now, Cam?" she said as she started to drive away.

"Yah, I think I'll take a nap now," he replied.

Chapter Seven:

The Picnic

The next week at school was a challenge for Cameron, as well as Kevin and Bill. After their experience with the light gate and the taste of virtual reality in the demo they were shown, they couldn't wait to have another chance to try it; they just couldn't get their minds off of it. Cameron was just tired of trying to figure out what Sonja was doing and how he would be involved in whatever she had in mind.

There were tests in class that all of them were convinced they failed; they couldn't focus on studying or homework in the evenings. Ironically, though, they were all doing rather well in their studies. They were doing extremely well, so well, in fact, that their teachers suspected they were cheating.

The following week, new classes were offered at school as mini courses, giving the students a taste of some subjects and career choices that were not offered in the regular junior high curriculum. There were independent studies as well, and one of them was video game design. Of course, Cameron, Bill and Kevin took it, but they were surprised to see that Sonja was in the class, as well.

The class started out with all the math that was involved and as it went on, Sonja got bored. She obviously pushed her pencil to the floor so she could bend over and whisper to Cameron, “Let’s go on a picnic this Saturday at noon.” Cameron tried at first to ignore her but relented and gave a nod. The week went by fast for Cameron, Bill and Kevin, most likely because they were really enjoying the subject matter. The weekend arrived and Cameron was hesitant about the picnic facing him on Saturday.

When Sonja came by to pick up Cameron, he was playing with Sandy in the front yard. Chuck was there and took Sandy and told Cameron to go and have a good time. He really thought that Sonja was more of a girlfriend than just a friend to him, and that made Cameron beam a little.

“Somehow food tastes so much better when you eat it outside, don’t you think? Making special food for someone is a very giving character quality; it shows that you care,” Sonja said as she set the food out on the table. “There is planning involved as well. What if it rains or there are a lot of bugs, or you haven’t found a good enough spot? Are you prepared for the conditions, and did you bring enough food? Giving of yourself in preparing food and planning for every contingency and eventuality are good character qualities to have."

"Why are you going on and on about it?" Cameron asked, raising an eyebrow. "I guess there will be some kind of adventure when we get to this place where you want to have a picnic."

"Well, don't sound so dismal. I thought that you liked adventures and such,"

"When I can choose it for myself, yes. But you have to see how these journeys into the unknown for me are like school tests, right?", Cameron asked.

"I think that this one will be fun for you and for me," Sonja said as they pulled into a small picnic area with large trees near a pond. "Have you ever read a story or seen a movie where you are so into it that you begin to think of yourself being in the scene and the things that were happening were happening to you?" Sonja asked while she spread out a blanket on the ground. They lay on it and looked up into the sky.

"Not lately. I guess when I was a lot younger, stories and movies were more real to me in that sense," Cameron said. "And I remember having bad dreams after watching scary movies on TV."

Sonja resituated herself on the blanket, looked at Cameron and said, "Well, that's what this scenario is like only in full virtual reality." With that, the blanket that they were on began to ruffle, and they both fell through. They fell about three feet down onto the stone floor of an ancient Greek temple ruin.

"Did you ever see the movie *Jason and the Argonauts*, Cam?" Sonja asked. "This is the scene with the blind man and the Harpies."

"Yes! That's one of the movies that gave me nightmares. The Hydra and the sword fight with the skeletons," said Cameron.

From where they landed, they could see the columned perimeter of the temple with long, stone capstones all around. When Cameron lifted himself up on his elbows, he could see in the far opposite corner an old man seated at a small stone table where two women in blue, flowing gowns carried large plates of food. There were fruits and large pieces of meat and steaming vegetables along with a pitcher of something to drink. What a feast that they set down for him!

There on the fallen stonework were two weapons. One was a bow with a quiver of arrows and the other was a fine, two-edged sword with a round shield made of some kind of metal.

Cameron, looking down at the weapons, said, "I suppose we're to use these in this scene."

As they continued to watch, the two women placed all of the food and drink on the table for the old man who appeared to be blind as he groped around for it. Both of them got on their hands and knees and scurried over behind some carved stones that hid them from the action on the other end of the temple as winged creatures began to swoop down at the man.

The winged creatures didn't seem to bother the two women, but as soon as the old man tried to grab the food, they came down on his arms and snatched away the food that he had grabbed from the feast table. He shook them off and picked up a rather large leg of some kind of animal and started to eat it furiously; almost instantly, they came again, darting in to snatch it away with their sharp talons just as he would have bitten down on it.

"So, Cameron, do you remember this from the movie?" Sonja asked. "These are the mythical Harpies that wouldn't allow the old blind man to eat as punishment from Zeus. Jason and the Argonauts came up with a plan to trap the Harpies in a giant net that they draped over the top and sides of the temple enclosure. Since we don't have a net, we are supposed to fight the Harpies off with these weapons. Which do you prefer?"

Cameron began, "So, although I really appreciate the battlefield support of range weapons and have used them from time to time, I prefer to go into a melee with a good sword most of the time. As a berserker, if it's an option."

With that, Cameron jumped up, grabbing the sword and shield and started running across the temple floor, leaping over rubble and overturned ancient furnishings strewn over the area. He jumped to the table just as one of the Harpies overturned a platter of fruit; it went all over as Cameron sliced through the midsection of the beast, cutting him in half. He got a good, close-up look at them in that instant. Their heads had the look of a raptor, but their eyes were almost human. Bright green blood gushed out all over the floor as the two halves of the creature fell, *splat!* to the base of the table. Cameron didn't remember the blood being green in the movie.

"Who's there?" cried the blind man.

"We're here to help," yelled Cameron heroically. "We are friends that have come to get rid of these nasty Harpies for you so that you can eat."

"It won't work; it never works. All of my family have tried, and all of my family are dead. Zeus will just send more and more. He has an endless supply of them. I am cursed," he choked out. "Leave me, please. I might get a good, long meal out of your efforts, but Zeus will come back at me with a vengeance when you are gone. I can get what I need to survive without your help, thank you, though just barely."

"We could take you away from here with us," Cameron offered as he continued to hack and slash away at the unrelenting Harpies.

"That has been tried as well," he said. "My saviors have always been killed by some plan of Zeus, and I find myself back here after all is said and done."

Cameron tried to think of options and began to speak as if he were repeating a quote, "The source of the problem has to be taken care of first if the problems themselves are ever going to be resolved. What is the cause? What can we do then to appease Zeus so that he will let you go?" he asked. "There must be something."

"There needs to be a substitute, someone willing to take my place in the torment," said the blind man, sobbing and desperately grabbing for more food and something to drink.

Cameron turned back to his task as more and more Harpies fell by Sonja's bow. It was hard for him to see himself offering what the man required even if it was a virtual reality situation. If he did it just to fulfill the design of the lesson, would it be sincere? Would it be sufficient?

Cameron jumped down from the large stone that he was standing on and grabbed up the man, slight which he was, and carried him out of the temple. Sonja came over to tend to him as Cameron ran back in to sit down at the table, slashing at the beasts that remained while trying to eat the feast that was left on the table. The scene slowly faded, and they found themselves back on the blanket, gazing up at the clouds.

"Wait," Cameron yelled out. "What was my score?"

"Don't worry, Cam. It was a good one, I'm sure," said Sonja. "That was a rather unique move. Not many finished it that way before."

"Thank you, but now I'm starving. Virtual food doesn't have much flavor," he responded.

Sonja began bringing out the food that she had brought packed in an honest-to-goodness wicker picnic basket like a relic from the past. It was a late lunch that consisted of fried chicken, potato salad, coleslaw and pickles. For dessert she brought an apple pie, store bought but good, nonetheless.

"From what I understand, this is the quintessential picnic meal. What do you think?"

Cameron couldn't answer right away because his mouth was already full of chicken, but he vigorously nodded his head.

"That was truly a selfless, self-sacrificing move, Cam," Sonja proclaimed. "I'll tell you; it has happened before, but rarely. And never with such quick determination. You received the full score for this venue."

"I think that because I was so hungry when we fell into it, the determination came from my stomach," said Cameron. "Isn't that what is meant by intestinal fortitude? I don't know, but it's sure good to be able to enjoy good food and good friends in freedom. This was a very good idea that you had, and I'm so glad that you brought so much food."

After lunch, they both lay down again and just stared at the sky. Cameron's mind was trying to rest, but there were questions that needed to be answered.

"How would you say that Bill, Kevin and Peter did with the sample last Sunday?" he asked. "Will they be acceptable trainers some day?"

"What makes you think that's what we have in mind for them, Cam?" asked Sonja. "I just want them to be able to play ball when we get a full team together."

"Sure, that might be what you're after in the short run, but I don't think that you would be putting so much time and effort into it if there wasn't something more," Cameron surmised.

"Well, you're right, Cam. We need all the trainers that we can get," said Sonja. "But we also need to have good team players, and who better than your friends. Peter is the only one that you know that I am training to be a trainer, but these others, besides Bill and Kevin, you have never met before, and part of the scenario is to evaluate how well you all play together on a team."Cameron was satisfied with that explanation, and he started to rest again until he realized what she was saying.

"I know that you will tell me soon enough, Sonja, but did you notice that I didn't ask again who the 'we' are that you always talk about?"

"Yes, I noticed, and I appreciate that. Yes, I will tell you all that I can soon. Thank you, Cam," she said.

"One other thing, Sonja, before I have to get back home and do my chores."

"What's that, Cam?" she said.

After an uncomfortable hesitation Cameron asked, "Do you know that I think that I love you?"

"I'm not at all surprised that you think and feel that way," she said. "I have fond feelings for you too, although I can't say that it's love. I'm sorry if that's not what you wanted to hear, Cam, but I have grown close to you more in the cause we can share in, not the physical and emotional attraction to one another. I just wish and hope that you will have more passion for it like your father."

Another uncomfortable hesitation on Cameron's part and he finally said, "I appreciate your honesty, Sonja," he began. "And maybe there is still time for your fondness to grow into love, but I'll have to see my dad face to face before I can say that the passion he has is something we can share in. It's not that I have any disdain for the human race, mind you; it's just that there has to be that confirmation from him that all of this is necessary. No offense."

"None taken, Cam, and I anticipate that day coming soon," she said, confusing Cameron with his wishful thinking about them on the one hand and his desire to see his dad on the other. Then, out of the blue, "Do you read a lot, Cam?"

Cameron thought it very odd for her to come back with such a question, but without missing a beat, he said, "What do you think, I'm a nerd. Of course, I read a lot. Maybe not many mainstream books, but I have quite a library."

"So, that's what we will do before the baseball game," she said.

"Do what?" he asked.

"Go to the library, silly. That will be the last venue before the baseball game. Sound good?" she asked with a lighthearted tone.

With an awkward halting voice, Cameron said, "Sure, that'd be fine. Next weekend then?"

"That'll work. Now, I better get you home before Sandy has an accident," she joked.

The ride to Cameron's was kind of quiet, and when he got out of the car, Sonja said, "I'll see you in school, Cam. Bye."

Saturday night was exhausting for Cameron. He couldn't keep his mind in the game, and he kept lagging behind, slowing the others down. It was as if he wanted to explore more instead of accomplishing the objective of gaining loot, leveling up and killing the monsters along the way. He became enamored of the environments of the settings where the game took place and its graphics rather than its function and goals. Combat went well to the point of him taking on the enemies with such vigor that you would think he was playing a single player game. After the battles he would just sort of meander through the environments looking at the graphics.

Sunday, Cameron slept in very late.

Chapter Eight:

The Library

On Wednesday in the school cafeteria, Cameron sat with Sonja, and she talked as if nothing intimate had been shared between them. Other than talking about classes and their weekend plan to go to the library, it was all strictly platonic. Not even a mention of his father.

When Saturday came around, they met at George's for pizza first and then headed to the library.

"There are so many stories and ideas, questions and answers, imagined and real-world places here. The riches of human contemplation written down for all to read. A building filled with the collective knowledge of mankind. What an elaborate undertaking to begin to know even a fraction of it," said Sonja.

"I could write a book," said Cameron.

"What could you add to this collection of writing that would be profound enough to merit a place on their shelves?" asked Sonja, kind of snarky. "How many pages would your story take to tell? What would be the titles for each chapter? What would you leave out of the book because everyone could check it out and read it? Would reading your story draw us too close to the truth about who you really are?"

"You really know how to encourage someone, don't you?" said Cameron. "Don't we all have a story to tell? Aren't they all important? I think you should lighten up on me."

"I know, Cam. I just got carried away with the magnanimity of books, sorry," she pleaded.

They went into a room where the after-hours book return slot from outside along the sidewalk was located.

"I want us to just stand here for about thirty-five minutes so that when we return, we will be right here," Sonja said.

Every so often, the clunk of a book or two would startle them as people used the overnight return slot. They looked at each other rather awkwardly at first, and one and then the other looked away to stare at something on the wall or at the floor or just off in space. Cameron thought, what do we really have in common? Was there nothing she wanted to talk about?

"Sonja, what have these lessons been leading up to? I know that you have some interest in me personally even though you have other 'students' that you're doing this with. What is it all for?" asked Cameron. "I like you; it's been weird, though."

Sonja looked him in the eyes and said, "You would have to ask that now. I have a good, long answer for you, but we will be in the venue before I can explain it all now."

"You make it sound so official and business-like. Who are you really?" asked Cameron.

"I am just Sonja. For you, I can explain objective one at this point in your development," said Sonja. "We have come far enough for you to be able to make a decision whether to continue to the end or not."

"You made that sound pretty doomsday. Care to elaborate on 'to the end' for me?" asked Cameron as another book clunked in.

"Okay, so when we went to the ball field to play catch, it was to measure your acceptance of the VR method as the proper way of training you. Your experience with VR games and such proved it to be the right choice," explained Sonja. "Some have to have a more analog approach to their training."

"To tell you the truth, I can't understand or figure out how it's done without a headset, and the time lag thing is way over my head," answered Cameron. "How many are being trained?"

"We will go into much more detail when we are done here tonight. I will tell you as much as I can sometime soon," she said. "We can talk about this next experience when we return. I think it's time."

With that being said, Sonja took out a bright yellow gemstone, and the light gate opened between them. They checked the time (it was 8:43 p.m.), and they both went through the gate into blinding brilliance. Instantly, the bright, white light changed to inky blackness, and Cameron sensed that he was falling. Not feeling any anxiety from the sensation, he was more intent on what he was seeing in the dark. There were books, thousands of them. Some were titles that he knew, and yet he was aware of all the titles as if he knew them as well, even of books that he had never heard of before.

Some of the titles he noticed that he had read were *The Lord of the Rings* by J. R. R. Tolkien, *Nineteen Eighty-Four* by George Orwell, *To Kill a Mockingbird* by Harper Lee, *Lord of the Flies* by William Golding, *Brave New World* by Aldous Huxley, *The Bible, The Canterbury Tales* by Geoffrey Chaucer, all of the *Harry Potter* series by J. K. Rowling, *The Wind in the Willows* by Kenneth Grahame, among many others. He wondered how he was able to take the time in his short life to have read all of the books that came to his mind; it was so overwhelming.

In the distance Cameron saw someone come into focus as the platform on which this someone sat moved independently of the level on which Sonja and he were standing. It was Peter sitting at a small round table reading from some large book. The book was larger than any he had ever seen before. The whole scene was set on a round disk floating close by.

“Peter, what’re you doing here?” Cameron yelled as he tried to step onto the platform where he was sitting. He got no reply. “Why won’t he answer me, Sonja? It’s as if he’s a million miles away, but I know that he’s close enough to hear me. I can’t get over to him, either” he added as the disk floated out of his reach. “I never pictured him quite like that. He looks kind of like an egghead holding up such a large book in front of him.”

“Cameron, have you never taken the time to talk with him, to find out what he’s into?” she asked. “I don’t mean to sound corny, but if you would take the time to ask, you would find out that he’s an open book.”

“Ha ha, very funny. Is he even able to hear me in here?” Cameron asked as he squinted to see where Peter had floated off to. “No matter now. He’s floated too far away.”

“Peter is just here as one of the characters for the lesson, Cam,” Sonja explained.

“I’m not sure how I’m supposed to score points in this scenario yet. Will it become apparent soon?” he questioned as he roamed around in the dark trying to see what would show up next.

The dark void began to change. Cameron sensed that there was movement in the darkness, but he couldn’t feel it. He tried to focus into the distance but with no light and nothing for light to have incidence on, he couldn't tell how far away anything was. There was nothing in the void.

"Why don't you sit down, Cam, and be patient. It will come into focus soon enough," said Sonja who was now sitting on a comfortable chair. As she patted the air next to her another chair appeared. "Here, have a seat."

He could see it but nothing else around it. The space was still blackness without floor, walls or ceiling. When he took his gaze off the chairs and Sonja, he lost his bearings and began to feel a slight disorientation to the extent that he thought he would fall. It felt confusing as he wasn't sure which way he would fall. He didn't know which way was up. Cameron had to look back and regain a focus point before he sat down. As he sat there for a little while, he began to feel better, and it was like sitting in a movie theater waiting for the feature to start.

An immense view screen or opening began to come into focus and get lighter. The image was of an aerial view as from a drone looking down on a small town nestled between the foothills of two mountain ranges. The scene slowly zoomed in to reveal a futuristic architecture. There were large, tall buildings clustered in the middle surrounded by shorter ones as you moved outward until the view came to zoom in on a modest, small business called "Aspire to Greatness".

"What's this about, Sonja?" Cameron questioned as the scene continued to zoom to a closer view.

Sonja turned and looked into his eyes. "Please be patient, Cam.

It has just begun. I can't tell you what the scenario will be like. It's not the same for everyone."

They both turned toward the scene and noticed that they were at street level in front of the entrance to the building. The sign over the door read, 'Ideas to Change the World.' Without noticing it, they discovered that they were totally engulfed in the venue as the view portal or whatever it was, placed them into the environment. They were sitting on a bench across the street from the building. The environment surrounded them now, and they could interact with it. People were walking up and down the street wearing the most unusual clothing imaginable. When Cameron looked over at Sonja, she was dressed to fit right in, as was he when he looked down at his own attire.

Cameron stood up and examined what he had on. The clothes fit loosely but comfortably. The shirt was made of some kind of shiny material, yet it seemed to breathe well. It had three-quarter sleeves that flared at the cuffs. His pants were made of a different material that felt light, but he could tell that it was tough enough and durable. The legs ended with gathers at the ankles. The shoes were form-fitting to his feet with just the right amount of arch support, and they felt tailored especially for him. Sonja had on the most wonderful, wispy sort of gown that could pass for evening wear yet practical enough for office-type, work clothing.

They walked over to the entrance of the building, and, to their amazement, the door was unlocked. They both thought that it was later than it really was and that the place should have been closed for the night but apparently it wasn't. They walked into an immense lobby with lounge-like furnishings and a wet bar across the way. The main counter for the receptionist stood in front of a wide hallway that had many doors to the different departments of the building. One was 'Propulsion and Transportation'; another was 'Green Energy'; and another 'Diamond Cloth' and so on until the imagination became tired of trying to figure out what they could possibly be. The one that intrigued Cameron the most was simply called 'Water.' It brought to memory the cut-short conversation Cameron had with Sonja just before they entered the light gate for the Museum. Interestingly, the subtitle for the department was 'Graviton Displacement Well Drilling.' The conversation had to do with his possible future.

"Sonja, what are you showing me here? If I go in here, will I see myself?" asked Cameron, in a freaked-out tone.

"I don't know, Cam," she said. "Let's go in and find out. It's the only way you're going to know."

They went in and past a reception desk that was vacant and into a back room. It was an elaborate lab with bright lights, counters with all sorts of equipment strewn over them and a man standing behind one of them. He turned to them, and Cameron took a double take as he recognized Peter. Somewhat older, but it was him, unmistakably.

"Welcome, Sonja and Cameron; so nice you could come for a visit," Peter said without mentioning their obviously younger appearances. "Come and look at this latest version of the drill gun we have developed for the remote mountain regions."

The portable drill kits were very sleek and compact. They were not too large and heavy to carry or travel with. They would fit in a checked bag or could be carried on a flight.

"Hiking into the jungles or remote villages of the Himalayas to bring clean water to the people there will be easy with these," said Peter. "A lot of the work that we do here has to do with graviton particles, you know. Something that you gave me the idea for way back in the early 20s, remember, Cameron?"

Hesitatingly, Cameron answered in halting words, "I, I haven't been to the early 20s yet, Peter."

Sonja whispered, "Cam, you should play along. The program will adjust to your dialog,"

"There are seemingly endless ways in which we can use the natural properties found in nature to better our world and our lives. Gravity, light, gluons from both the strong and weak bosons from nuclear forces. These are the materials that we study and apply as ideas are discovered to change the world and its environment," Peter explained. "The seeds of these ideas came from you, Cameron. Your friendship is very precious to me."

"Well, thank you for saying so, Peter, but—" Sonja poked him, and he changed what he was about to say. "We have to be going now. Thank you for giving us the short story of what Aspire to Greatness is all about."

When Cameron and Sonja left through the door to the Water department, they entered a street in Ware at night. They found themselves on West Street, in front of Ware Junior/Senior High School.

There were lights on inside which was strange at first, since the school was normally closed by this time in the evenings. There was some kind of event going on, most likely to do with sports.

Sonja said, "Why don't we go in and check it out? There must be some reason that we find ourselves here." She noticed the school sign all lit up. It listed a few events with dates, and even though they didn't know what the date was, the girls' basketball game for the Ware Indians versus the Turners Falls Thunder was tonight. "Well, that clears that up, ah, Cam?"

Next on the list of events was the science fair for 2016, Saturday, 11:00 to 2:00. "We are three years in the past based on this sign, Cam," said Sonja.

"I remember this, Sonja. We don't have tickets for the game, but I think that we can sneak in to have a look at the science fair projects in my old classroom. The one that my group had was great," said Cameron, and he had a sudden realization.

"That's where I first remember meeting Peter!" he yelled. "He was in my class. We were assigned to a group project. Peter, Kevin, Bill, some random girl that I can't think of her name, and myself. It was three years ago. This would have to be it."

They went into the school, and as they made their way through the halls to his old classroom, Cameron said, “That’s probably why Peter was at the beginning of this scenario. He helped us on the project, but the day of the fair, he was nowhere to be found. We had a real problem with the project that Peter, no doubt, fixed. He most likely came in the night before and did it for us, and we never saw him again after that. He wasn’t very popular in school, same as us. That is why we were all put together in a group. I’m sorry to say that he wasn’t missed much.” Cameron looked down in shame. “I don’t even think that any of us asked what had happened to him.”

“That next week, Peter was placed into Woodland Academy, the private school. He is highly gifted, you know,” said Sonja. “He needed a more concentrated, personal teaching experience so that he could thrive.”

They reached the classroom where all of the science projects were set up, ready to be displayed the next day. They were lined up, waiting to be taken into the gym. There were the usual volcanos, solar system models, plant diagrams and terrariums. There were rocket models, geography sculptures that showed the layers of the various kinds of rock strata with meticulous labeling, but all seemed rather simple and uninteresting. Then they came to the project that Cameron’s team put together. It stood out from all the rest, even alongside the very impressive, giant dinosaur diorama that seemed to be so out of place among the other,
lesser exhibits.

Their project was supposed to be a working model of how

antigravity was to be achieved. It demonstrated a beam of light energy directed down from a mockup of a fantasy spaceship model that, in theory, would cause it to hover and float above the ground or water. It could also be propelled in any direction and at any speed. The text that surrounded the display was notes on the theory, attempting to explain, in layman's terms, how a working prototype of such a thing could be built.

"The spaceship was supposed to be supported with wires. Dry ice was going to be used for effect, and we had a small flashlight to shine down from inside the ship, but Peter made it all work," said Cameron, as they approached the project. At that moment, he saw him. "There's Peter."

They caught him taking the spaceship apart and placing a small contraption inside. He snipped the wires, placed it on the ground of the diorama and flipped a switch on top of the machine-like object. Then he put the ship together again and stood back holding a small remote control up, pointing it at the display. He didn't acknowledge that Cameron or Sonja were in the room at all; it was like they were shadows from the future.

Pushing one of the buttons on the remote caused the ship to rise and hover in place. The light from the flashlight was on as if it were the cause of the hovering, and Peter set the remote down on the edge of the project and left.

"So that's what happened. We never could discover how Peter had done it. We entered it in the fair the next day and won, but Peter was gone," Cameron said. "After the fair was over and we went out for pizza to celebrate, we came back to get our project, but it wasn't there. We were told that it was confiscated by, we were told, authorities. To this day we don't have any further information about it. All I know is that Peter turned out to be a genius."

They both looked at the project as it continued to hover there, and the band music from the basketball game began to filter through the halls to reach their ears.

"We should go, Sonja," said Cameron. "We need to get back to reality."

"Cam, this will be your reality someday soon. It's time for you to understand that," Sonja said very seriously. "I can tell you who the enemy is, Cam, but you will think that I am pulling your leg. But, yes, we should leave the venue now."

They both made for the doors of the school, closed their eyes and held their breath and when they would have been stepping through the exit, they found themselves in the library once again. They were still staring at each other as they both opened their eyes. It was awkward for Cameron, and he looked away. Looking down at his watch he discovered that it was 8:28, fifteen minutes before they left. The clunk of a book being returned startled them, and as they stood up, Cameron remembered what he had thought just before they went into the light gate—What do we really have in common? Was there nothing she wanted to talk about?

Then he remembered that she was going to tell him more of what these lessons were leading up to. He had more of an idea now, but she said that she would explain it. “What is your good, long answer, Sonja? What have these lessons been leading up to?”

“Well, Cam. Let’s catch our breath first,” she said. “That was quite an adventure.”

“Most of what we experienced was in the head, and I can see much of the answers from it,” he said with confidence. “You said that you would explain what Objective One was. It seems that my decision to continue to the end is based on understanding that.”

Another book clunked in.

“The enemy has a name. It is collective; they are Cacodemons,” Sonja finally said. “Cacodemons are evil spirits or demons. Cacodemonia is a form of insanity in which the patient believes that they are possessed by an evil spirit.”

“That sounds pretty supernatural to me. Wouldn’t there be more obvious evidence if demons roam around attacking people?” said Cameron, skeptically.

“Cameron, the patients are the victims, and they not only *believe* they are possessed, they *are* possessed. The spiritual world is invisible, but the evil influence is very evident in the world around you.”

Cameron was shocked that she used his full name. It must be important. However, he thought, Why would I take her to be such an authority figure in my life? It might have something to do with her knowing my father all these years.

“Objective One is knowing the nature of the enemy and being willing and able to engage them. The lessons help you to be able to see when evil is the principal object in the way, as a manner of speaking. Selfishness is the first and persistent manifestation of evil, but you need to be trained to determine if it is self-serving or to further a greater, righteous cause that might be hidden. Evil can manifest itself to look righteous.”

“I don’t see why this information couldn’t be explained up front. That’s more along the storylines of some of the games I play. Now you’re talking. But I have to admit that I’m a little scared if this is real.”

“It’s real, Cameron,” she said. There was that full name again. “Remember when I told you that your future would be like a game of chess? It was in relation to the deeds done for the benefit of humanity. I mentioned the graviton particle displacement drill. Has that been confirmed in your mind that I was right? Many places in the world need clean water for drinking and cooking.”

“Yeah, I remember that now, Sonja. Thank you,” Cameron said bowing his head down in shame.

“So, you see, Cam,” Sonja said with a tone of seriousness. “These lessons are training you to be able to observe situations that need adjusting. The whole new generation needs to be able to think through and devise strategies for success; needs to know how to get things on track rather than just complaining about how things are. You have been given the inside view of the problems in these scenarios and how the solutions might be beneficial for more than just the problem at hand. In the world, problems demand an outside view of the solutions as well. We set things up that force you to be involved intimately with the problems, hoping that you will come up with strategies that consider the overall benefits of how the solutions will work, in order to put more than just the immediate situation right. Not just the initial incident, but the bigger picture; this training is far reaching to ensure that the solution will be broadly effective. When that goal is reached, it means that you are ready."

"Is that what you meant by the end, then? The end of the training for me?" Cameron asked.

"I'm afraid so. Then it will be time for me to leave," she said with finality. "But don't despair; we have over seven million trainers activated in the world at this time."

"All of this has been going on behind the scenes for some time, then. How could we not have known?" said Cameron with astonishment, sitting there with his head in his hands in the small library of one of the small towns in the country.

"I think it's time, Cam," said Sonja.

"Time for what?" Cameron asked as he lifted his head up.

"Time that we all got together for some baseball. Even if it's for just one inning, it will give everyone an opportunity to play and work together as a team. We need to meet the others that are in the program from surrounding areas as well. None of you have met them yet," she said. "How would that be, Cam?"

"If it will usher in 'the end,' I'm all for it."

Just as they were ready to leave the library, another book was dropped off into the after-hours return slot. Being curious, Cameron lifted it out. The title of the book was *Gravity*, by Tess Gerritsen. Oddly appropriate.

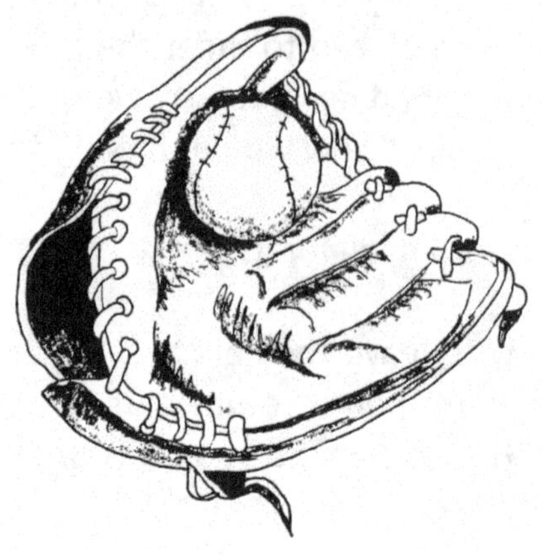

Chapter Nine:

Baseball

"What is a Baseball Glove?"

A baseball glove is a beginning and ending: a boy's first sure step towards manhood: a man's final, lingering hold on youth: it is a promise ... and a memory.

A baseball glove is the dusty badge of belonging, the tanned and oiled mortar of team and camaraderie: in its creases and scuffs lodge sunburned afternoons freckled with thrills, the excited hum of competition, cheers that burst like skyrockets.

A baseball glove is a thousand-and-one names, and moments strung like white and crimson banners in the vast stadium of memory.

A baseball glove is the leather of adventure, worthy successor to the cowboy's holster, the trooper's saddle and the buckskin laces of the frontier scout; it is combat, heroics, and victory ... a place to smack a fist or snuff a rally.

Above all, a baseball glove is the union of father and son, boy and friends, man and men; it is union beyond language, creed or color.

Cameron's eyes popped open, and Sandy bounded off the bed. It was 7:15, very early for him to wake up on a Sunday. Something about what had happened yesterday, combined with his dreams, made him want to go to church this morning. His mom went fairly regularly, and after having a quick breakfast and witnessing the shock of her hearing that he wanted to go, they were on their way. The message that day had to do with the unseen realm of evil and demonic activity in the world. Cameron didn't think of it as coincidence but rather confirmation of what had been going on all this time. The passages from Scripture were not unfamiliar to him, having been brought up with the Bible from a very young age. Verses like I Peter 5:8 where he was warned to be sober and vigilant because his adversary the Devil, as a roaring lion, walks around seeking to devour him caused him to wonder why the Devil would be the slightest bit interested in him.

The next week would be filled with sleep-deprived nights and days of pondering how he could have gotten tangled up in what he was realizing was the reality of evil in the world. How could he be a leader against such a force with the task of vanquishing it? Cameron had a lot of questions about Sonja, such as what it was like where she was from?

It was decided that the next Saturday, Sonja would gather all of the players in for a game of baseball at the old, abandoned ballfield north of Eddy Street. Cameron told Kevin and Bill about it, and Sonja would let Peter know. They didn't know who the other players could be, so they were all looking forward to finding out. The game was set for 1:30, and there would be a lunch provided around 12:00 where they could eat, talk and get to know each other a little.

The week was a fog as far as school went and Cameron felt like he had drifted through it as if someone else was in control instead of him.

When Cameron got to the ball field on Saturday, Peter and Bill were already there, waiting.

"How long have you been here, you two?" asked Cameron. "Eager to play or just to have the VR experience again?" He smiled and looked around at the field. "I've been in this venue before. It's amazing."

"We met up and came together about a half-hour ago," said Bill. "I think it's a little of both for us. You said that we didn't need any gear, right?"

"That's right. Everything is there in the scenario," answered Cameron.

Just then, Kevin came riding up on his bike with Sonja not far behind. Cameron had never seen her on a bike before. He would always just see her suddenly showing up or coming over or he would meet her someplace. This was new. As they were all standing there together, Sonja began, "You might be wondering where the others are. They will be arriving inside the venue from three other locations around town and some from other states."

They all just looked at her dumbfounded and then, talking in hushed tones among themselves, "How is that possible?"
said Bill.

"This will make the greatest multiplayer platform game system in the world. I wonder how far players can enter from," wondered Kevin out-loud.

"It would, no doubt, be way too expensive for any of us to be able to afford," said Cameron.

Peter just stood there, not saying a word.

“Shall we go in, guys?” she asked, as she took out her holalectrum. The zipper of light formed from top to bottom as one by one, they entered through the gate as it opened, Sonja taking up the rear. Kevin, Bill and Peter were awestruck with the modern looking, sparkling clean ballpark they entered, nothing like the shabby, rundown park of their reality. It was early November in Ware, but in the venue, it was mid-July.

The infield was set up with tables that held a feast for the whole group. There was a podium with a microphone set up at the head of the tables and the grass was so green that it looked almost fake. Of course it was, but it had the feel and texture of real grass and smelled like summer.

They stood waiting for the other players to enter the venue. It wasn’t long before the gate crackled and spit a little. Then, three guys came through that none of the four had ever seen before. Next, there came a girl with long, flowing blond hair. After that, the gate began to sputter and shoot out sparks just before another guy came jumping through. He was a tall African American with his hair in long dreadlocks. Cameron thought that he knew him from someplace.

“Kevin, isn’t that Jerod Woodhouse from our school?”
Cameron asked.

“I believe it is. Hi, Jarod, we had no idea that you were a part of this,” said Kevin. “Aren’t you a senior now?”

“Yes, I am a senior this year,” said Jerod. “This has been a long, strange journey for me.”

Bill went over to the three guys that came through first and found out their names and where they were from.

"New Bedford. I'm Mike Carter, and these are my friends, Brandon Finch and Bradly Knight," he said.

As the two stood talking together, another girl came through the gate. She was young and wore glasses and had short, black hair. Peter took a special interest in her and went over to introduce himself.

"Hi, my name is Peter Nithala, I attend a private school here in Ware called Woodland Academy. Where are you from?"
he asked.

"Hi, I'm Vicky Greenbough. Believe it or not, I come from a smaller town than this, Warren, just about three and a half miles southeast of here. I'm homeschooled, but I test much higher than the national scores," she said in a humble tone. Peter didn't get the impression that she was boasting at all and felt that she was as shy as he was. Entertaining the idea that they could hit it off as a couple, Peter began to be slightly hopeful with his newfound friend. He thought to himself that it would have been almost impossible for him to have met anybody that he could relate to or get to know in a personal way if it hadn't been for this training course with Sonja.

Sonja maneuvered around to the head of the table at the podium, getting ready to speak into the microphone as the group was mingling about. With such a small group, it seemed kind of silly to them to have a mic, but it was a large venue and the acoustics were bad in the stadium. There were only eleven in the group so far, twelve with the arrival of the last one.

Sonja tapped the mic, and the thump, thump sound got everyone's attention.

"Well, there's one more coming, but it might take a minute," Sonja said. "When we are all here, I will make introductions, and we can eat and get to know each other more."

Cameron went over to the blond girl and said, "So, I guess we'll get to know each other better soon enough. My name's Cameron Adams. Have you played much baseball?"

"I'm Samara Miller, good to meet you. I'm on the softball team at my school, but I love playing baseball with my friends," she said. "This is very unusual to me because usually I am in a completely foreign or alien environment when I go through the gate. I know that I am in my hometown and that helps, but I was told that this venue is in Massachusetts, I'm from Vermont and just a little nervous about this."

Another sputtering and spitting of the light gate and the last guy came through. He looked more like a football player with muscular, broad shoulders and short, curly brown hair. The light gate zipped closed from the top to the bottom and vanished with a loud snap. Sonja stood on a chair and began the introductions.

"This is Samuel Pettit; he goes by Sam. It took him a little longer to get here because he came from Michigan," she continued. "Closer to home, we have Jarod Woodhouse, a senior in our local school. If you could stand when I introduce you so everyone can see you, please. Next, we have three from New Bedford, not too far away, Mike Carter, Brandon Finch and Bradly Knight or Brad to his friends. Vicky Greenbough comes from Warren just a few miles southeast of here and last we have Samara Miller, from South Burlington, Vermont."

Everyone just sort of looked at each other for a few minutes.

"So, this is our team. Get to know each other for a time as you eat this delicious food," Sonja said. "We will continue with what your positions will be, and I will introduce the opposing team. You might want to start thinking about a name for your team as well."

Bill, Mike, Bradly and Brandon made their way to one end of the table and started in on the food as they talked as if they were old friends already. Kevin and Jarod joined them on the other side and Sonja came over and sat down with Cameron and Samara, filling in next to Bill. Peter and Vicky held back and continued talking as Sam sat down by Kevin and Jarod.

The table was filled with all sorts of food and drink that most were leery of seeing that it was a virtual reality experience. But to everyone's surprise, it had real flavor as if it were actual food. They began eating and talking baseball with each other.

"MVP 2005 for PS2 was the best baseball video game ever made. Still haven't gotten rid of my PS2 because of that game alone. At least once a year, I'll go on a week-long binge playing it," said Kevin.

"MVP 2007 has great pitching and batting controls," said Jarod. "You pull back on the right stick to ready your swing, and it loads up for the pitch. If you do it too early, you lose most of the pop in your swing. Do it too late, and you'll be swinging after the ball smacks the leather of the catcher's mitt. I do like the '05 version, though."

"Video game baseball was big among my friends back in Michigan," said Sam. "The schools were too football centric in their sports programs, so the baseball teams that I was able to join didn't stand a good chance of having quality coaches. Fill in math and geography teachers and not any preparation for good competition with other schools. I was never in a winning series."

"Michigan has never been known for their baseball," said Bill. "The Tigers, right? Although they did win in '84," he added.

"Nothing compares with a real game of baseball, though," said Samara. "Wouldn't you agree? This simulation is exciting, but I know that it won't compare well with the real effort of playing and teamwork."

Sonja spoke up, "That's the real exercise here. Teamwork. Those principles cross over into everything that's worthwhile for the human race to endeavor to accomplish. The hope of effective teamwork skills has no ultimate limit for every discipline of life."

Kevin tried to bring it down to the bare essentials of the game by saying, "A perfect inning is a no hitter, and the credit can only go to the pitcher for his skill in knowing which pitch to make for the batter-up on the other team. There is some teamwork if the catcher knows something about the batter and can signal the pitcher, but mostly it is a one-man accomplishment," Kevin continued. "Now, a well-played inning where teamwork is fully employed, that's a beautiful thing to see. If someone gets a hit and a base or two, it's up to the whole team on defense to do what they do best to keep the runner from making it to home plate. The pitcher may suddenly shoot the ball to first or second or third as the runner leads off to steal a base instead of pitching to the batter, and a baseman or shortstop must be ready and alert to catch the ball and tag the runner out if at all possible."

"Yes, it's so nice to see a well-executed, precision triple play," said Kevin.

Sonja spoke into their big talk about the fine points of baseball by saying, "To the extent that you understand teamwork in a baseball game, you must understand the bigger picture of life and the team that you build for expertly implementing change in the real world. To make the plays that are called for to see the human condition better to the point of, and for the sake of, survival. We don't want to see the other team win. They are gaining skill and becoming better and better at what they do. I fear that mankind is on its third strike with the bases loaded, but I have confidence that you and your teams can turn it around. Home plate can be defended and taken back. Things might go into extra innings, though, and I want you to have the skills and stamina to see the game through to the end and come out the victors."

They all just looked at her with amazed expressions on their faces. "That's the strangest pep-talk I have ever heard," said Kevin, looking over at Cameron. "Is she serious? It feels like we have to play to win back the planet, not just to have a good time."

"Well, we just can't let them intimidate us. We have a better cause to win," Cameron said in response. "We just need to play our best and take every opportunity to observe the details of their plays, as well as have a good time doing it."

Everyone went back to their individual conversations as they continued eating.

"Cameron, could you grab Peter and come over here?" Sonja asked. "I want to talk to just the two of you for a minute."

"Sure, I'll just be a second," Cameron answered as he put his hand on Peter's shoulder. "Sonja wants to talk with us."

"Okay, but smelling all that food is making me hungry," said Peter.

When they went over to where Sonja had wandered off to, she began to explain. "The other team is your enemy. The other members of your team will not get a true look at them but you two have the ability to see replays of the game in real view.

That means that you get a glimpse of the true enemy that exists in the world and how they may appear in other forms."

"Well, that's kind of messed up," said Cameron. "Isn't that a little unfair to the rest?"

"I will let them know after the game, but right now, consider it serious training, almost a final exam for the two of you," she said.

"What do you mean by 'other forms,' Sonja?" asked Peter.

"For instance, they may appear to you in the real world as someone from your past like a bully or someone that you had a fight with at some time," she explained. "In some cases, it might be a real threat like a criminal that you see on the evening news. They want to catch you by surprise so that you are not able to think clearly or to make you feel like you can't deal with them on your own to scare you off. Sometimes they may appear as monsters that you thought could never exist. It's times like those that you need to rely on your team and not hesitate to bring them into the fight as it were."

"I don't get how the replays are going to be a thing that only we three get to see. When is it supposed to happen? We will all be playing, right?" asked Cameron. "If we step out and view the plays, what are the rest going to think?"

"That is something that you have puzzled over before, Cam. How can we go through a light gate and come out up to thirty minutes before we went in?" Sonja said. "This is a dynamic we employ here for the purpose of reviewing the plays while the rest of the team is suspended in time. Please don't ask me to explain it to you. I can, but you would have a hard time understanding it."

"That's convenient. I would like you to explain it someday, even if you think that it would be hard for me," Cameron said.

"I appreciate that, and I may. So, when plays are made, we have the option of being allowed to see them like an instant replay. The opposing team will appear as their true physical manifestations, which are demons. You will see that they sometimes act as if they are anticipating what the play is, where the ball will go, who will respond to the play and who will hesitate or ignore it, deferring it to someone else and so on," she told them. "They will be right there before the play is made. In the game, you will see them making for the play but in the replay, they are already advanced to its conclusion. That's the nature of your true enemies in the real world."

"We better be getting back to the others, they might be curious about our being huddled apart from them," said Peter with true concern.

"No, they won't even know that we were away. You will see how this works," Sonja said. "One more thing. Other times their team will let ours make a play and mess it up just to let us see how unskillful we are. We get discouraged and they gain an advantage over us. This is only baseball. We can fail in here but think of it as training for the real world. The skills that you will need to hone in relationships and in dealing with people in business and in every other encounter are vitally important when you move to engage the enemy out there."

Sonja assured them that there would be good examples of how the Cacodemon's nature plays out in the simulation and let them rejoin the rest of the team. They went back to the table, and Peter sat down to eat by Vicky who had saved him a place. Cameron sat at the foot of the table and started asking for the food to be passed to him. There was fried chicken, mashed potatoes with gravy and roasted vegetables with some incredible smelling herbs and seasoning on them. Cameron filled a plate and started eating as he listened to their conversation. He couldn't believe what he was eating.

"Add this to the list of I-don't-know-how-they-do-it, but the food is incredible. I can taste it, and it tastes great. If virtual means that it won't put any weight on you, I want to come here for all my meals," said Cameron.

The talk was turning from baseball big talk to the game at hand.

"Okay, so who is the other team that we can't let win?" asked Bill as he stood up from the bench. "We will need to know all that we can if we have any hope of defeating them."

"You say that we need to know our team members well to ensure a well-played game, but we have never even met these seven new players. I mean, other than Jarod from our own school, and we only know him as an upperclassman," said Kevin. "These lessons are the only thing I would have in common with him. Cave dwellers rarely mingle with their own class, let alone the upper class."

"You sure do paint a dismal picture of yourself. There are a lot of students that know you, Bill and Kevin, a lot better than you might imagine," said Sonja. "Most aspire to your academic achievements. Just because none of you like attending, and often duck out of, awards ceremonies, you are known and appreciated for what you have accomplished."

"Is that why you chose me and my friends? Do trainers have to be nerdy smart for the program?" questioned Cameron.

"No, in fact, Jerod and some of the others are way below average in their academic achievements," she said. "Some have artistic abilities in art and music, so there is a factor of creativity that is involved, even strategy, but I am not sure of the whole criteria for selection. Anyway, we should make a great team, and this should be a really fun game."

Cameron shouted out, "Listen up people. I think that we need a team name. Any ideas?"

"I think we ought to be called the Salamanders," said Sam without much hesitation.

Many in the group were asking how he came up with a name so fast, and why the Salamanders?

"Is that because it would make a cute mascot or logo?" asked Bill with an adolescent accent. "The mere image of the Cacodemon's logo would destroy our mighty Salamanders."

“I don’t think that our namesake’s image would have any bearing on which team is better,” said Cameron.

“Still, I think that our team’s image would go a long way in giving us confidence for the win, don’t the rest of you?” Vicky questioned them.

Sam kind of held his head down and addressed the team.

“Back in Michigan there were two guys that died. They were in this training same as we are.” Sam explained. “They were well loved by most of the school that I attended. Two new guys slid right in and took their places. You see a salamander is capable of regenerating their lost tails, and I just saw those friends as part of the body there. I have given it a lot of thought.”

After bowing his head down and thinking for a few minutes, Sam continued.

“Any one of you may come to a place where all of those working alongside of you fails or comes up short of what your expectations are of them. Some may fall away and that is all right if you consider that on the whole, as a body working together to accomplish the goal of eradicating the Cacodemons from the world, just like a salamander grows a new tail, you will gain new members and continue on. I’m not saying that it will be easy. Just like losing his tail, it hurts. It hurts really badly. You need to be patient with each other and willing to welcome new members that may have the exact skill or talent that is needed to accomplish the tasks that fit into the overall plan.”

"I couldn't have summed it up any better myself, Sam," said Sonja. "Let's finish up and get to it, what do you all say?"

The feast was over, and all of the players had as much as they wanted to eat. When they stood up, the table vanished, and there they stood wearing the green and yellow uniform of their team, the Salamanders. They all turned their heads as a flash from the scoreboard proclaiming the Salamanders versus The Cacodemons. The stands were suddenly filled to capacity with loudly cheering fans. Sonja stood at the head of the group and began to give a kind of pep talk to the team.

"Just so you know, there will be game announcers that will mention you over the loudspeakers throughout the game as if you were famous major league players. Try not to be distracted by them. It's all part of the lesson," said Sonja.

The whole affair seemed like so much more than just a friendly game of baseball. The team took on a proud look; this is something they would like to have invited their families to watch. Now they knew that it was not just for fun, but a training session that would give them insight into how to deal with the true, evil threat in the world.

"We want to see team players in this game today," Sonja started. "Cooperation may mean the difference between winning and losing. We all have our groups of friends that we interact with to different degrees. Some we just want to talk to and bounce things off of once in a while. And there are others that we want to be more involved with; we want to do more with. We need to be team players in this game and in life. This game has rules just like all other games; there is the goal of winning. The principle of good sportsmanship, how we play the game and what we are willing to contribute to it, what we are willing to get out of it, we take from how we live our lives. Life is not a game, but it has rules and objectives. We can contribute and expect to get a lot out of it just the same. Just as we need to be all in with this game of baseball, we need to be all in with life. We are running out of time, and I don't say that to frighten you but to encourage you that we have a chance to win in life also. We need to be able to trust our teammates even if we just met them and just started to get to know them. If we are all in it to win, that is the common factor that can bring us together as a good functioning team."

Everyone looked soberly at each other giving nods of agreement and approval which seemed to indicate their willingness to do their best in the game as well as in their lives.

After that Sonja looked down at some notes she had on the podium and began to call out the positions for the game.

"Okay, here are your positions, and they will also serve as the batting order for when we're up. Number one is Brandon, number two, Kevin, number three, Bradly and number four will be Jarod. I'll be number five and Cam, you will be number six. Now in the outfield, Samara, number seven, Peter, number eight and Mike, you will be number nine."

"I don't know how much good I will be to the team since I don't even know what these numbers refer to," said Samara in a somewhat frantic tone. "What does it mean that I am number seven?"

"Samara, don't worry about it, we are here to help you along," explained Sonja. The team gave reassuring glances to her. "Number seven is left field. One is for the pitcher, two is for the catcher and three through five are first, second and third base. Six, that's me, it's for shortstop. Seven through nine are for left, center and right fields. Does that help?"

"It sure does, just don't be surprised if I ask again as we go along," she returned.

"Let's play ball!" Cameron shouted as the loudspeakers crackled to life.

"Good afternoon ladies and gentlemen. I'm Ben Cranston along with Don Crow and here we are with Game Seven of the 2058 World Series with a full house on such a wonderful day for a baseball game. The Ware Salamanders versus the Boston Cacodemons."

"Yes, it is, Ben. It's a beautiful day for a ballgame."

The ball field was in Ware so; the guest team was up at bat first. So, the Salamanders took the field. Brandon took the pitcher's mound while Kevin, donned in catcher's garb, took his place behind home plate. The lineup for the Cacodemons looked brutal. As the first batter approached the plate, a lefty, Brandon looked for a signal from Kevin.

"Brandon Finch will pitch for the Salamanders today. He's had a good series, six for nine with three runs scored. I would say his last seven games at Citizens Bank Park have been at a torrid pace."

"That may serve to be rather disturbing, hearing professional sounding announcers throughout the game," said Cameron.

As previously decided between Kevin and Brandon, the basic signals for the pitcher would be one finger for a fastball, two fingers for a curveball, three for a slider and four wiggled for a change up. The type of fastball would be up to Brandon, whether a four seam or two seam. Any other pitch would be up to him as well.

Kevin flashed his index finger and motioned toward the batter indicating an inside fastball. When this happened, Brandon was given a pitch option screen suspended in the air off to the right of the mound. It was discovered that the interface for using it was by just looking at the one Brandon wanted and with his eyes fixed on it, he just nods his head. An inside fastball it would be, and he found that he could pitch like a pro. The ball went right where he wanted it, to the right side of the strike zone and the batter hopped back and strike one came up on the scoreboard.

After two more like that, Harold Markham, the first batter up for the Cacodemons was out.

“That looked too easy. Don’t you think, Peter?” Cameron asked. “If that is any indication of how the game will go, we are sure to win easily.”

“I don’t think it will be too easy. I think that it may be a strategy to get our confidence up,” Peter answered.

“Good observation, Peter,” said Sonja. “That can be a common misjudgment when you are in the thick of it out there in the real world.”

As the second batter, Archie Pepper, came up to the plate, Kevin sized him up. He thought that he would be an easy strikeout because he was small and skinny and held the bat too far out away from his body. Brandon threw an eephus, thinking that he could trip the batter up a little but when the bat made contact with the ball, it drove just to the left of the mound and sailed all the way to hit the back wall. Samara and Peter both went for it and fumbled each other trying to get hold of it. Peter finally got it and shot it to Sonja, the shortstop and the runner was stopped at second.

“Well, that shakes things up a bit,” said Cameron. “If we aren’t careful, they could get him home.”

"He should have saved that pitch until after a few fastballs first. That pitch is supposed to be used when the hitter is expecting something else," Peter explained.

"Next up, Carl Vanmar. He's the centerfield for the Cacodemons and he's six and two with a 4.09 ERA, big strong lefty. Carl swings and misses at a fastball."

Back to the fastball, Brandon thought he could put a few to Carl and then sneak in a change-up or curveball to get him out. It worked with Archie getting to third base and with the next pitch a double play sent the Cacodemons to the field.

That was it for the Salamanders and they all run in to take their places for batting. Brandon went to get a drink and grab a bat. He was up first.

"It's the bottom of the first and there's Bob Garrison taking the mound today for the Cacodemons as they look for their first series victory since the end of April. The youngsters had a chance to have balls and cards autographed before today's game. That's a cool moment. The kids out there are meeting their favorite players."

"Wasn't Harold Markham supposed to pitch for the Demons Sonja?" Cameron asked. "He was first up."

"You will find, Cam, that in this game, just as in real life, Cacodemons do not always follow the rules," said Sonja.

Brandon started to warm up in the bullpen as the other players began figuring out the lineup for batting and started taking practice hits. They all felt like professional athletes and started to act like ones as well.

“I know that we are assisted in the game and enhanced by the program of the venue, but doesn’t it feel so real?” said Bill. “I mean just look at all those virtual people in the stands.”

“It is amazing what these little adventures can accomplish, and I’m always amazed at the detail of the different environments that I’ve found myself in,” said Cameron. “It’s just that Sonja always makes it into a lesson so it isn’t as fun as it could be.”

“I heard that,” said Sonja. “Life isn’t all fun and games like when I first met you. All your life consisted of was making time for your games. Well, here’s a way to get involved with more than just your two friends at least, and for a real purpose on top of that. You’re welcome.”

The loudspeakers began cranking out the announcer’s voices again:

“Now the Salamander’s lineup brought to you by Exuberant Tech, it will change the way you experience life. A lively look for the Salamanders because Bradley Night is batting third today. Jarod Woodhouse batting cleanup. Sonja will bat sixth for the salamanders. They face Hellickson who is five-three with twenty-four strikeouts. Not a strikeout pitcher. He had a real rough month in May with an E.R.A. of 7.04. So, Ben, he's hoping that the Cacodemons can turn the page on the month of May and start fresh here in June, boy it was a tough month.”

“Boy, that is kind of unnerving to hear about yourself as if you were a major league baseball star,” said Bradly.

“You can say that again, but I think I like it,” said Mike.

“Here comes Brandon Finch batting first for the Salamanders, a lefty from New Bedford along with his two hometown teammates, Bradly Knight and Mike Carter. So much talent from the same little town. Harold Markham will be catching for the Cacodemons.”

“It’s a real privilege being able to bat first on a team that doesn’t even know me and my friends. Thank you,” said Brandon to the others as he jogged out to home plate.

The team acknowledged him all in their own way with nods and thumbs up and ‘You got this.’ The first two attempts were balls and then on the third try his bat hit smack on to drive deep into right field where the sun obstructed the fielder to get Brandon all the way to third base. The team couldn’t believe it and the stands went deafeningly wild.

“That was quite a play for Brandon, and I think his teammates are a little surprised. Seventy-eight Kevin Brady, who started the first game of the series with a three-run rally with two outs, will be the focus area. He’s always played a tremendous game. In the field and today, as Don mentioned, he's bound to have some tough chances.”

The pitches came with measured regularity with not much

variation to the point that Kevin was a little nervous to know what might be next. The fourth pitch after three balls and Kevin swung. He pounded the pitch deep into left field. The outfielder couldn't get it in his glove and Kevin touched first base. He saw that the ball was missed by the shortstop and was able to round to second. The fans went wild, and the rest of the team couldn't believe that he was able to make second batting Brandon in for run number one.

On the replays, however, Sonja, Cameron and Peter witnessed something not short of diabolical. They saw close-up expressions on hideous, contorted faces that gave them every reason to believe that the plays were meant to be made just as they had been. But for what cause? thought Cameron.

Bradly Knight is up next, and the first pitch is fouled. The next one is a ball and on the third pitch, Bradly connects and the ball pops up and is caught as he starts out for first. Kevin is tagged sliding into home for a
double play.

"We have got to get better than this if we hope to have a chance," said Cameron. "Is it because we viewed the underside of their previous plays?"

"No, they have no idea about that in here," Sonja assured.

"You mean these are the real things in here?" Peter asked, astonished.

"They are only avatars, I promise you," Sonja said. "You will need to do better in the game. Sorry."

"Two outs, one run and here's Jarod Woodhouse at bat. There's the pitch and Jarod slams it straight into the right field's glove. That's out and the second inning is about to begin."

"Well, there we go. Maybe we can shut them out in the field. If we only get one run, we can make sure that they don't get any," Peter said. "That sounds kind of impossible though, now that I say it out loud."

Although the day was bright, cool and breezy, there were moments where dark clouds rolled through threatening to rain if only for a short time. Usually, it was at times where the Salamanders had made a good play or were about to or making a home run or striking out one of the Cacodemons. It served to reinforce the idea that it would be bad for the Cacodemons to win or get a foothold toward achieving success. The correlation was subtle but effective in a subliminal training module. Even the weather can encourage or discourage the team in the ongoing struggle. It's what's on the inside that counts, Cameron thought.

"All of a sudden, it's kind of a cloudy day, but we'll get past that as Hellickson is ready to go. Here's the first pitch of the afternoon. That's in there for a strike and someone calling to Markham. It's no balls and one strike. I think he heard something from Brandon Finch on that pitch right out of the shoot."

"You could make a living right there down in the zone."

The top of the second inning was a closeout for the Cacodemons giving the Salamanders a clean slate going into their second time at bat.

Sonja is up first and knocks the first pitch into the stands giving her a homerun. Cameron just cannot get a hit and strikes out. Next up is Samara. She strikes the first and gets a ball before slamming one to left field which is not picked up in time to stop her from getting on first. Then Peter, whose mind is not fully on the game, grounds out giving Samara one more base. Mike makes a base hit which gets Samara to third and now with two on, Vicky Greenbough who just can't seem to get a good hit. After three balls she pops up to be out with Samara and Mike on base.

Next, Sam is up to bat. So, Samara is on third, Mike is on first after Peter's grounder got him out and Sam steps up to the plate. He looked like he was holding a broomstick instead of a Louisville Slugger. As if the spectacle was a good enough distraction, Samara steals home as slick as you please. The first pitch was right in the sweet spot, but his swing completely missed.

"That ball would have gone into orbit if he had connected with it," said Bill. "This guy is massive."

"Strike one," came the umpire's decree. The next pitch was a little lower and to his right, but he connected, and the ball went screaming just right of center field only to be caught by the right outfielder. Third out came up on the scoreboard, and Sam walked back to the dugout with his head down. When he got there, his teammates shouted encouragements like, 'Good effort,' 'Way to smack that ball, Sam,' and 'That's all right, Sam, these guys are monsters,' that last from Cameron brought a look from Sonja and Peter like he had just let the cat out of the bag.

"Don't worry, guys," he whispered. "They won't take it literally."

"That's the end of it," said Sam with a dismal tone. "One run."

"That's two runs, Sam," said Cameron. "We are ahead, get out of the dugout. We have a long game in front of us yet. You know it's only a game, and a simulation at that, but you're going to have to be more resilient in the real fight and not let little things get you down. Remember, we are all here for you."

With Cameron's lighthearted encouragement things went along smoothly all throughout the top of the third inning completely shutting out the Cacodemons.

"So, Don, that brings us to the end of the third chance for the Demons to get a run up on the board. We've seen some real defensive plays by these Lizards."

"That's right, Ben, the Cacodemons are heading out to the field with nothing."

The team is feeling good after their efforts in the field as Brandon takes the plate for the first pitch of his third time at bat for the Salamanders. The first pitch came so fast he didn't have enough time to gage it and swung wild.

"Oh, that's a dandy. Boy that really snapped in there," said the announcer.

After three more came whizzing past he was almost dizzy with the fast turnaround of pitches. Brandon steps back from the plate and steadies himself to give his best effort on the next pitch, it could be a homer or an out.

"Two balls two strikes another curve-ball below. Garrison, hasn't walked anybody today and his fans said that he's allowed only one hit, an infield hit."

It's as if, suddenly, everything begins moving in slow motion as he steps back to the plate and the ball comes at a good speed for him to hit smack on the sweet spot. The ball is sent to left field and Brandon takes off for first. Then there is the familiar sound a glove makes when the ball is suddenly caught. He's out with that sound in his head.

Kevin slaps Brandon on the back as he passes him on the way to home plate for his turn at bat. With dogged determination and a great desire to follow-up Brandon with a good hit, Kevin stands away from the plate and gives his arms some practice with the bat. The first pitch is put where Kevin wanted it and with great force he sends the ball straight down through the first basemen.

"There's a line smash base hit and now here's Bradly Knight.

Knight is the type a hitter you don't dare make a mistake on, and even if you don't make a mistake, he's strong enough to hit anything out of the ballpark."

With Kevin on first, Bradly drives him to second with a base hit of his own.

"They bring up the grand slam kid, Jarod Woodhouse. He's had two homers and six runs batted in the series. He had twenty-one homers and led his team in runs batted in during the season with ninety. He's had one out of nine against the pitching of Garrison and that was a home run. That was the only run that Garrison permitted in this series."

Jarod drives Kevin home with a rising right field hit. Run three for the Salamanders.

"Another run by Kevin and a base hit from Jarod and the Salamanders now made their first threat with two on base, Bradly and Jarod."

Sonja comes up to bat, swings and misses the first pitch for a ball and Bradly steals third. Her second swing connects and is caught by right-fielder Charlie Strang. It's quickly thrown to home and Bradly is out. That is three outs and the Demons come running in.

As the team walks out to take their positions, Sonja reminds Cameron that it's only a game yet the skills that the Cacodemons are developing is part of the lesson about how they will progress in the real world as they interact more and more with people.

“That was a well-executed double-play and I have run this venue many times before. Even the virtual representations are getting better,” said Sonja.

The first pitch of the fourth inning was fast and right in the strike zone. It was as if Brandon was trying to give them a hit. The ball was sent straight back at him and smacked him in the head dropping him instantly to the mound. He lay flat on his back while Kevin, Bradly, Jarod and Cameron came running to him. He was staring up into an overcast sky and it looked as if he was holding his breath. His eyes were wide open and no sooner had the group decided to carry him off of the field, he fizzled and vanished.

“Just one victory for Bob Garrison, that big E.R.A. He'll be about ninety, to ninety-two. Very good change-up. Curveball, which I would love to see him use more and his cutter is starting to come along as well.”

“He was talking the other day about making sure he uses his fastball with a little more ability to spot it and maybe that would get everyone off their change-up. It seems like people are sitting on his change-up over the last several starts.”

It was as if the announcers hadn't seen or wouldn’t acknowledge Brandon getting hit. The banter between them continued on as if nothing happened.

“Time now for our Nissan keys to the game. Then, Don, kick us off.”

"You just said it, Ben. He's going to use a fastball more. I'd like to see him use the fastball more. These guys are sitting on the change-up. Even when he hits down in the zone, they are looking for it and getting it. You can use the fastball and command it."

"To me it's about momentum. I've talked about that a lot. Win one more today, you'll have taken the series from San Francisco and go to the next series and keep the momentum going and win that series. Before you know it you're back where you want to be."

"The Cacodemons are just waiting around for a new pitcher. They don't even care about what just happened," said Bradly.

"Remember team, it's only a simulation," said Sonja.

"To face facts, what did just happen? Was Brandon just hurt or was he killed? Or did he just want to leave the venue, just go home? It did look like he was holding his breath. That is the way you leave," said Kevin. "He could've said goodbye at least, you would think."

"One way or the other, they didn't show any concern or compassion. They didn't know what happened," said Jarod.

"But you forget that they are just virtual. There is no person to them, and I believe that is supposed to show us what the real enemy is like after all," said Cameron. "What better way to exemplify them."

Cameron had the impression from the Cacodemons that they wanted to appear benevolent but had an ulterior motive for everything they did or said. He felt as if they were always plotting. It was almost as if they were playing at being human but were just not that good at pulling it off.

They decided to put Bill Drake in to pitch the rest of the inning.

The bottom of the fourth and Cameron is up first. He just can't seem to get the big question out of his head of whether Brandon was killed or just went home. It would clear up a lot of things for him if he knew.

Carl Vanmar walks over to talk with the pitcher, Bob Garrison and then returns to first base.

"Vanmar and Garrison are not discussing the weather down there, which is beautiful by the way. Woodhouse tips the ball to all fields. Oh, fly ball Vanmar, hay, he almost falls, and it went over his head. Two runs are going to score if something isn't done about it. The same thing almost happened earlier in the game to Jarod Woodhouse and now it has happened to one of the greatest defensive center fielders in baseball, Carl Vanmar. If we start it over, something happened to his other buddy."

"Why are they calling him a center fielder when he is playing first base?" asked Peter.

Bill spoke up with, "It just doesn't seem to matter to them what the rules of the game are, they just play whichever position they want to."

Cameron regains his focus and is able to hit a rising left field ball to get him on first. Now Samara comes up and gets ready before approaching the plate.

"I would have caught that one if I was at first," she shouted to Cameron, heckling Carl.

With pride and confidence in her skills as first basemen, her hit ends up being caught for the first out of the inning.

Trying to keep it lighthearted, Cameron shouts as he runs back to first, "You're such a fine first basemen, now you just need to polish your batting skills."

Peter is up next and after using up everything in his arsenal gets a base hit. Two strikes and three balls but he gets on sending Cameron to second. Mike hits a drive just right of center and gets on as well, pushing Peter to second and Cameron is tagged by the shortstop as he heads to third. That's two outs for the Salamanders. Next in line is Vicky who hits one to left field. It's picked up and shot to home plate just in time to get Peter out.

That should have been it, three outs, but the ball was quickly thrown to the shortstop, Frank Cumberland, as Mike rounds second heading for third. Frank misses the tag on Mike, so he throws the ball to Bob on third. For some reason the dust churned up by all of the action between second and third is so thick that it is hard to see just what happened.

The noise that was heard by everyone was unmistakable. The ball hit Mike in the head and there was a blue sparkle which lit up the dust cloud for an instant. When the cloud dissipated, and with the crowd in the stands cheering like mad, Mike was nowhere to be found.

Peter motioned to Cameron, and they stepped out of the game with Sonja to view what the play looked like outside of the program. The dust cloud was rolled away to reveal the true situation. To the horror of Cameron and Peter, the Demons shortstop Frank Cumberland, appeared twice as large and was hideous. His, or rather Its, demeanor was intentional as the ball was thrown with incredible malicious force right at Mike's head. The look in the monster's eyes was that of satisfaction when it knew that the player was out of commission. Peter and Cameron just stared at Sonja with fear on their faces.

"This is how the enemy plays the game I'm afraid," said Sonja. "They are, how you say, hell bent on taking people out of the picture."

This served to sober the two up and encouraged them to rally the team on to do their very best and keep up their spirits in the face of all that had happened.

"I'm sorry for the stark reality but the real situation is desperate, and all of this is supposed to make you aware of the true battle that has been raging on for hundreds of years," said Sonja. "I will fill the rest in on this after the game."

The next three innings were straight forward, uneventful and without any great plays worthy of mention other than the maintaining of evenly matched skills affording no further runs and not much happening between outs. The gameplay was intense, but all met with equal determination and effort to stop each other from advancing.

After each inning the three would step out of the game and review the plays that had the fiercest struggles and see how well the Salamander's skills improved. As well, they observed how the enemy struggled to maintain its balance, which was more heartening in the face of the training and developing a fighting force for the real world.

"You know, when you think about it and looking back, I believe the last three innings were the best of the game in spite of the fact that neither team advanced," said Cameron. "It was quite the grudge match, and it took a lot of intestinal fortitude to maintain an equal standing."

Back in the dugout just before the team took the field for the eighth inning Cameron told the Salamanders as much and gave quite a pep talk going back into the game. The virtual crowd seemed to be over-exuberant towards them when they did come out onto the field to take positions.

Bruce Andrews is up first and hits a heavy, high arching ball right down center making it halfway to first before it is caught by Peter. The call is made by the announcers, but Bruce just keeps going. The ball is snapped to Bradly on first and just before it is caught Bruce smashes into him sending him flying. For a moment it seems like there is a gap in Bradly's travel to give the visual impression that he has faded out of sight for a distance and when he comes back into view, he vanishes just like Brandon did on the pitcher's mound.

"I don't think that I trust what I just saw," said Jarod.

"What did we just see?" questioned Vicky followed by Bill and Sam. They were all sent into confusion as to what was going on. The replay didn't seem to offer anything too much different from what happened except that Bruce turned out to be in the form of a local criminal that had been on the news a lot lately along with the look in his eyes as he mowed down Bradly.

With that Sonja set things into perspective for the team.

"Brandon Finch, Mike Carter and Bradly Knight, they were important players in this game as each one of you are important to the real task at hand when we are finished here," she said. "This is training after all, but sometimes the training needs to be so true to life that we have to acknowledge our true feelings and understand whether we are up for the life we have been made aware of. Sometimes I wish it didn't have to be me that makes that known but we all have our parts to play in life."

They got back into focus on the game. Jarod catches the next hit tagging Bruce out at second and fires it right to first where Sam takes over for Bradly. Charlie Strang is out at first. The very next hit is caught by Bill on the mound and Harold Markham makes the third out. It seems that nothing can deter the Salamanders from redeeming their losses. As they head for the dugout, they get some fiendish looks from the Cacodemons.

The Cacodemons took the field as if they were soldiers manning their posts. The first pitcher, Bob Garrison, takes the mound like he is a gun emplacement.

Sonja delivers an incredible show with each pitch from Bob. First a ball then a foul and two more balls, two strikes and a hit spiked to left field.

Dave Carmichael misses the catch, and it goes bouncing into the outfield. That gives another home run for the Salamanders.

“Watch this now. He positions for this spike see, and he nearly fell down and that cost him gagging the ball plus very rarely has he ever misjudged the ball out there but when he stumbled on his way, it threw him out of his path, he couldn't get back, so the ball sailed over his head and the Salamanders now have four runs coming into the ninth.”

Cameron, Samantha and Peter all three strike out after Sanja’s dazzling play but they all go into the last inning with great hope and determination.

“So, Ware leads four to nothing. Next is Dave Carmichael, the batter, he’s nothing out of two. The curve is a beauty over the inside corner. And he’s out at first base, tagged by Sam Pettit.”

“This is starting to look very promising guys,” said Sonja. “If we close this out that’s a win.”

"Bruce is up next, and I can't get the image of what he really looks like out of my mind," Cameron said to Sonja in a hushed tone. "Man is he big."

Bill did a good job pitching but he asks for relief after he lets Bruce get on first.

"Two balls and a strike as he singles. Now they brought up Woodhouse to pitch and the first ball screams hard, directly into center field. Peter Nethala slipped as he started for the ball and missed."

Charlie Strang goes to the plate. He is a lefty, so Jerod is having a little bit of trouble getting his pitches adjusted for him. The controls for right-handed hitters are more familiar to him.

"That's a long drive to right center field, Greenbough on the run can't make the play."

Charlie gets on first and Bruce advances to second just before the ball gets to Bill who swapped with Jarod for pitcher. Harold Markham tries a bunt which hasn't been used in the game so far, and makes it to first base as the ball is thrown to third preventing Bruce from going home.

"A base hit, another batter on pushing the bases loaded up as Archie Pepper comes up to the plate."

Jarod knows what this next play could mean for the game as well as what it could mean for the training program. He felt some pressure and almost wished that he was playing without the aid of the program so that he was more in control, but he winds up for the pitch and lets it fly.

The ball is popped up and caught by shortstop Cameron who shoots it home and Bruce is tagged out as well, double play and that's the game.

"A clean play off Woodhouse and that's the Salamanders dugout, it's now a happy place."

The Salamander's dugout was a very happy place as the team high-fived each other and celebrated with Gatorade and sunflower seeds.

"I am very proud of the way you have all played together as a team today - very effective I must say," said Sonja. "The goal was not only to win, but to learn and get to know each other in a team setting, functioning well and able to enjoy the journey."

"But we lost some," said Sam. "How is that commendable?"

"Yes, I'm sorry about that, but those three, Mike, Brandon and Bradly, were not real. They were only simulations placed within the scenario as teaching tools," Sonja said. "You got to know them a little and they were gone. That will, no doubt, happen in the real fight as well."

"I just thought that after the unfortunate plays that they were involved in, they no longer wished to be in the game or the venue and went home," said Jarod. "It seemed like the coward's way out if you ask me, and now I'm glad that they weren't real."

“It seemed to me that Brandon was aiding the other team,” said Peter. “Are we to believe that some within our own teams will side with the Cacodemons? If so, whom can we trust?”

Sonja looked at Peter and then caught Cameron’s eye with an affirming glance. She had seen something special in how Peter could detect Brandon’s treachery.

“You see, Peter, when we have true purpose in life and can share in something much larger than ourselves, we have the ability to become unselfish. It’s a choice nonetheless, and if we make the right one, it is much easier to progress toward the goal. The enemy will offer whatever they can to take you away from the goal,” Sonja explained. “We need to recognize the needs of others on our team and see that they have what is necessary for them to stay on track with the program. Truth be known, there are so many in the world depending on our success. We must reduce and eradicate the increasing instances of evil triumphing over good in the world.”

The team just sat still in the dugout for a long moment thinking about all that had transpired during the game. The shock of finding out that Brandon, Bradly and Mike were simple VR characters was heavy on their hearts. Getting to know someone to a certain extent and finding out that they weren't even real seemed like cruelty to some.

"This has truly been a game to remember and now that you have seen who the other team really is, I think that you have gained the confidence needed to be able to face them in the real world," said Sonja.

"One question, though," said Vicky. "How will we be able to tell when we are up against a Cacodemon and not just the evil that men do?"

"Oh, you will know. That's a great question, though, since evil is rampant in the world. As long as you have your holalectrum with you, they will appear to shimmer, slightly out of phase," explained Sonja. "Kind of like looking through a bonfire. It's a very fast shimmer that you may not be able to see without your gems, but I know some that can do it, and with more training and experience, you may be able to develop the ability as well."

"Well, the main thing is to know that we can call on and count on other teams to help when we need it. Are we going to be shown how to proceed with projects and strategies for our defense?" asked Cameron. "It has to be more complex than a game of baseball."

"I have placed packages at your exit points for you to look through and study. There is a lot of contact information and maps of a network that you will be impressed with I think," said

Sonja. “I’m sorry if the incidents in the simulation seemed more real than you expected but this is serious business and the most important work of your lives, we need to make you ready.”

Many knew what Sonja was referring to when she said ‘we’ as they all had been going through the training. Cameron would fill Kevin and Bill in on the whole thing later when he started training them. He would tell them about the Rapah and the millions of agents for truth training human pods all across the world.

“Just like in this game, your opposing ‘team’ will either take you out or make you ineffective in your mission,” said Sonja. “So, whether that means death or just your inability to function with the skills you have been honing, that is their goal.”

The team members began to get ready to go, offering handshakes and hugs as they made their way to the pitcher’s mound where the light gates would be opening. When all was said and done, the group left through them one by one, except for Peter and Vicky. They went through together.

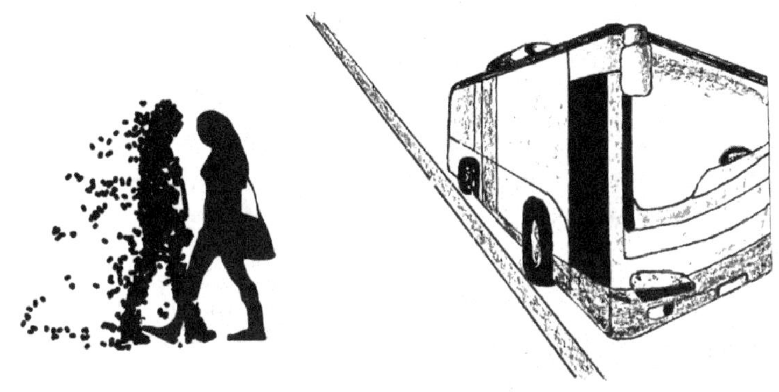

Chapter Ten:

The Mystery

The next morning Cameron slept in late. It was Sunday and he had no plans for the day other than the usual, and when he did finally wake up, he just lay there in his bed, basking in the victory of the night before. The greatest inning in the history of baseball. Sandy was at the foot of his bed and lifted his head up when Cameron looked down at him.

"There's my good dog. How you doin, Sandy boy?" Cameron said as he sat up and reached down to pet Sandy. "Do you want some breakfast and to go for a walk this morning?"

Cameron was thinking that he would give the guys a call and have them over for backyard breakfast when there came a knock at the front door. He heard his brother talking to someone that sounded like Sonja. He got up rather reluctantly and threw something on to go down to meet her with Sandy. Just as he reached the front room, Chuck was closing the door. As Cameron rushed over to snatch it open, Chuck kind of clotheslined him back onto the couch to the left. "She said to meet her at the ballfield around 10 a.m." Chuck was a man of few words. "And come alone."

"You didn't have to slam the wind out of me, did you?" coughed Cameron. 'That's great.' He thought. 'I can have the guys over for our backyard breakfast after all.'

Getting his wind back, Cameron hurried up and got dressed. He took Sandy out for a walk around the block and thought of what he could make for breakfast for the guys. Pancakes for sure, with butter and syrup, and there has to be good, spicy sausage. Scrambled eggs with onions, green peppers, and mushrooms, with rye toast. Coffee, strong, and orange juice, he thought. "How does that sound, Sandy boy?" Cameron said out loud. "Come on now, I know that you can read my mind."

When he got back home, Cameron sent out a text message to Kevin and Bill. He looked in his contacts for Peter's number but couldn't find one for him. He added a message, "If either of you have Peter's number, forward this invite to him as well."

Sandy followed Cameron into the kitchen and went straight to his water and then to his food as Cameron went about gathering up all of the raw ingredients for his massive, backyard breakfast. When everything was almost ready, all but the coffee, the guys arrived through the backyard gate. Peter came with them also; Kevin had his number.

"So, what are your plans for today, guys?" Cameron said as he brought the coffee carafe out and sat it on the patio table. Everything was set and the feast could begin.

"Nothing planned, maybe a movie if anything good is playing, and then just hanging out." Bill said. "Are we on for gaming tonight?"

"Something tells me that I will not be able to make it tonight," said Cameron. I have to meet Sonja around ten and I don't know what all she has in mind to do. I do know that I will have some answers by tomorrow."

"Thank you for inviting me over for this, guys," Peter said. "I'm glad that you have included me as a friend, and Cameron, please don't fault Sonja for what she has done in your life. It's for the good of us all. And for the world on the whole."

"Don't worry, Peter. After the library scenario, I have a greater appreciation for her and for you. Some kind of future genius you could be," said Cameron. "I don't know if the things we experienced will become reality or just that they could, but I'm almost all in at this stage. There are a few things that I still need to straighten out for my own sake yet."

As they went about devouring the fine breakfast Cameron provided, Bill said, "So, Peter, you will have to take Cameron's place tonight in the game."

"That will be fun. Let me know when," Peter replied.

After the guys left and Cameron was finishing up with the dishes, his mom and stepdad came home from church.

"Hi Mom and Dad. I just had one of my big, backyard breakfasts with the guys and I'm off to meet Sonja. I might not be home until late, is that okay?" he asked.

"That will be fine. You two are becoming quite the couple, is it getting serious?" his mom asked.

"I don't think it can, mom," he said. "Just something about it that makes me feel like it couldn't happen. I'll see to Sandy when I get home tonight."

Cameron started walking to meet Sonja rather than ride his bike. He needed the extra time to think things through. So much had happened in such a short time, he was a little overwhelmed.

As Cameron stepped out of the path through the woods from his block to the ballfield, there she was waiting at the entrance. For some reason, the light was very bright in the clearing of the old street in front of the field. Or maybe it was Cameron's imagination that he saw her in a more dazzling light than ever before. He was still quite infatuated with Sonja and ever since he heard her say to Kevin, "We're just friends," he had been trying to not think of her as a possible girlfriend anymore. At this point in what he perceived their relationship could be, he was trying to perceive what it had to be.

Cameron thought that as fun as the virtual worlds were, he was done being tested with lessons to learn and points to earn. 'And for what?' he thought. "Sonja, I'm not in the mood to step through to the virtual realm today and come to think of it, maybe not ever again. I need answers; this can't go on forever."

"That's all right," she said calmly. "We are finished with that part. Will you walk me to the bus station?"

Such a relief came over Cameron that he forgot how tense he was becoming from almost dreading the sessions lately.

"Please, don't get me wrong, Sonja. The ball game was the greatest time because it didn't feel like I was in a classroom, so thank you for that and for including my friends," he said as he began to feel the tension leave his body and mind. "Is this when I receive my score and you let me know what it was all about, what it was for? Are you going to meet someone coming in on the bus?"

"I can give you your score, and no, I am not meeting anyone," she said and went on to explain, "You see, Cam, it all boils down to this. Mankind has two basic needs. People spend their entire lives trying to fulfill them even if they don't know what they are; they are motivated to fulfill them. It is who you are. It is basically why you do what you do.

"The two needs are these: security, which is acceptance, and significance, which is purpose. People need to be accepted and to have purpose in life. You are accepted by your friends but not by others in school who call you all cave dwellers, right?" said Sonja. "Yet you have some acceptance. Could you do something that would cause them not to accept you anymore?"

"Yes, of course. But why would I?" Cameron replied.

"How would you know that what you did caused them to reject you? Do you know them well enough to keep your actions and words under control at all times?" asked Sonja. "And what would you do if you lost their acceptance of you?"

"I would find out why and fix it," said Cameron. "Or make new friends."

They continued walking and crossing street after street on their way to the little park next to the bus station downtown.

"That would mean fixing you, making a change in you in order for them to accept you again. Would you be willing to do that?" asked Sonja.

"What does all of this matter? What does it have to do with what you are training me for? If they accept me now, what is the problem?" asked Cameron with frustration. "Am I going to change or are they going to change? And why am I asking you? You don't know."

"I'm just saying that whoever you are or whoever you become, you will have the need for acceptance. Someone that will accept you no matter what," she said. "It may be a close friend, a relative, your spouse someday or maybe some authority figure in your life. It may even be your parents if you can believe that.

"You can go through life discarding friends and making new ones, but as soon as they get to know you well enough, what is going to keep them from discarding you?" "Why are you painting such a dismal picture of life?" asked Cameron.

"I am simply explaining the basic needs that mankind has," said Sonja. "When they are fulfilled, there is no limit to what can be accomplished, but acceptance is only half of the equation."

"I think that people need to accept me as I am. Why should I have to change for them to accept me?" asked Cameron.

"Well, in a perfect world you shouldn't have to. This is not a perfect world, and there is not a lot of unconditional acceptance around. The only sure source for that is with God," said Sonja. "Growth is change, and your environment changes you without your even noticing it until you look back to see who you used to be."

"So, you are trying to get me to experience these scenarios so that I will be predisposed to change as my emotions are exercised because of the way that people behave?" asked Cameron.

"You are not entirely wrong there, but you are not entirely right either. Human acceptance is based on trust much like divine acceptance is based on faith. We don't want you to have blind trust or blind faith. The other half of the equation is purpose, that which makes you significant in life. Do you know what that is for you, Cam?" asked Sonja as they crossed over to the park.

"Well, that can change. I think that would have to change from time to time," said Cameron.

"That's right, Cam. But what I'm talking about is the purpose which overrides what you do or who you are. It's the why," said Sonja. "If you find your purpose and significance in your job, what happens if you get fired? Marriage, what happens if you get a divorce? Collecting stuff and amassing many things to yourself and the warehouse that you store it all in burns down, even if it was for the poor and needy? What should be the overriding purpose of you, Cam?"

"To tell you the truth, I have never given it much thought," said Cameron. "Most of the games that I play have winning as the overriding purpose. If life were like one of my games, I would have the purpose of winning. With some games you need to gain points, some you need to survive and get the prize, and some are just a distraction."

"So, if that were the case, which scenario would your life take on, Cam?" asked Sonja. "It's not important since that is not the case with real life, but it is important to understand how you see yourself playing the game of life. Kind of like a starting point, do you understand, Cam?"

As they both sat down on one of the park benches, Cameron continued, "Well, I don't see life getting in the way as a distraction like I used to, but I don't see it as gaining points either. What could you trade them in for? That leaves survival. I think everyone in the world plays for that, but what would be the prize?" he asked.

"You have chosen life and surviving it as your overriding purpose. Your prize will be all of the friends and people associated with you that are saved as a result of whatever you come up with as solutions to the problems that plague humanity," said Sonja with a somewhat pre-recorded-sounding presentation of a voice.

"Now that was just odd, Sonja. What the hell?" said Cameron while looking slant ways at her.

"I know, I sounded like an infomercial host right there, didn't I?" said Sonja.

"I think that you are taking all the fun out of my gaming," said Cameron. "I will never think about games the same way again."

"You do know that there is more to life than games, right? It does take the fun out of life when you start to see it from a more mature vantage point, and just for your information, we are running out of time," she said. "The scenarios are finished; there will be no more venues for your training. It's all available for you to access from your experiences. So, you will need to take this training more seriously than you have been. I am trying to engage you on a level that you are most familiar with but only as a vehicle through which I can get you to most easily understand its importance."

Cameron went quiet. He didn't know what to say, sitting on the bench and staring off into space. Then, as if collecting and shuffling his thoughts, he said, "How can you know when the end will be? How is it that mankind will be responsible for the death of their world?"

Then he looked deep into her eyes and said, "I don't even know if I believe all of this. I'm too young for any of this to be a conviction if I did believe it, and I don't see how I can right now. How would I change to have enough compassion to come up with solutions or to be of any use in whatever solutions are found?"

"Please don't talk like that, Cam. I don't want to see your world laid waste; I have seen it happen too many times before. I believe in you because I believe in your father." she said. "Our research has indicated that there is a high enough probability for there to be enough time for your own people, especially the up-and-coming generation, to save your world. At this time, we have 7,859 active trainers in North America. We began the project in your year, 1976 with twelve individuals all the age of eighteen. Cam, your father is one of the original twelve."

"Wait, you can't mean my father," said a stunned Cameron.

"Well, I was hoping that I would not have to be the one to tell you this but—now take this calmly, please—the father you know is not your biological father," said Sonja. "Your mother did fall in love and marry Carmine, your father, but Carmine, your real father with the same name, was teleported away when you were five and a half years old."

It was all becoming too much for Cameron to take in. He just wanted to run away and forget what he was hearing. It did make sense of some of the thoughts, images and feelings that he had in some of the scenarios.

"Why was he taken and why didn't my mother tell me? Didn't he love us? He wouldn't have left on his own. How can I believe you?" Cameron asked through anguished tears.

"He did love you both. Your dad loves your brother and father as well," Sonja said in a calming tone. "He is so passionate for the success of the project and so valuable to it."

"You mean he's still alive?" asked Cameron. "I want to go and see him."

"Yes, alive and very well, in fact, in the environment in which we have placed him. He is 61 now and is wonderfully young minded. You have his look about you. You see, his mind is intact, but his body is not." said Sonja. "He was in a terrible accident that human medical technology could not do enough to correct."

"So, what? He has tubes and stuff and machines keeping him alive?" he asked. "I can handle that."

"No, in fact, you would think that he hasn't changed much since your memories of him. Cam, he is in a virtual state, kind of like me," Sonja tried to explain. "I hope that you can draw strength from his experiences to be sufficient to the task of leading and training the many initiates that we have activated for the end-games."

"Why did you call it that after you just explained that it was not to be taken lightly, like a video game?" asked Cameron. "Can I go see my dad?"

"I would love to say, 'yes you can,' but Cam, you have to finish up here first. He is working well with all of us right now," she said. "And he knows your progress. He has known you throughout your life."

"I am going to need some answers, Sonja. It's gotten to the point that I half expect to find a ribbon of light gate around every corner in my normal day," said Cameron. "I am finding it hard to separate what is real from these fantasy worlds you take me to."

"I promise you that there will be no more virtual reality test scenarios. The process is complete now for you. I wish that it could have been more straightforward, but I didn't develop the program; I am just one operative in it," explained Sonja. "For what it's worth, Cam, if you could only hear yourself talk now, you are not sounding like a sixteen-year-old high school boy anymore. Not by a long shot. You have gained wisdom beyond your years, Cam."

"You know, Sonja, if it wasn't for the fact that everyone else can interact with you, I wouldn't believe it. Why did you lie to me, though? You spent all this time getting to know me when you could have just explained the whole thing up front. I would have understood some of the technical parts, at least I would have been all right with what I was experiencing to be able to fill in the parts that I couldn't understand," Cameron said with tears still forming at the corners of his eyes. "Was I that far gone that you had to devise this elaborate scheme to get my attention? Who is behind this?"

"The simple answer is yes, you needed to be jolted out of your comfort zone in order to see what was right before your eyes. Most of the initiates are this way. The world has a lot of problems that you, and others like you, can solve if you were out in it and could focus on them," was her answer.

"But why would an alien A.I. CG even care about earth's problems?" asked Cameron.

"I am only CG on worlds other than my own. What do you need, Cameron?" asked Sonja using his full name. "What is it that you don't already have?"

Cameron didn't have to think about it for too long.

"Time," he said. "I need more time to do what I want to do."

Even as the words spilled out of his mouth, he heard how selfish they sounded.

"The world is running out of time, Cam; that's part of the reason why I am here," Sonja said with a little emotion showing in her voice. "We have seen worlds sink into chaos and war and utter self-destruction that have not embraced the training and heeded our warnings in time."

"For the last time, who are the 'we' you are always talking about?" asked Cameron. "And just how would the end of the world happen in your estimation? What does your probability caution against?"

"Cam, we are trying to help you, I am trying to help. We have seen it happen to other worlds. We have also seen success with the program working. It's like a delicate plant that needs nutrients from the soil, oxygen from the air and sunlight. If the flesh and blood beings were responsible to supply all of these things and they gradually stopped doing it, the plant would die. When the population of a planet begins to lose interest in the responsibility to maintain the health of their environment, the world's engine begins to slow down and seize up. That's just the physical world. It begins with the metaphysical and all that is referred to as the Spiritual realm. People become more and more selfish and greedy for what they think they need and go about living their lives just for that. But they are fooling themselves into thinking that their wants are their needs and if there is not enough for them and for you, then it's too bad for you. I have what I need or want, that is all that matters. There ends up being no concern or compassion for each other.

When their world begins to sink, they will climb on anything that floats to keep their head above water, even if it is you."

This was a lot for Cameron to take in, and he just sat there. They both stayed silent for quite a while until Sonja began, "So, that first day that I showed up in school, what was that like for you, Cam?"

"It definitely was a turning point. I'm embarrassed to say that I instantly had a mad crush on you, but I never thought that it would go anywhere. Cave dwellers are shy and don't manage social situations well," said Cameron. "Lack of confidence, not being in on the current trends, thinking that the rest of the world just can't see what we get out of the whole gaming thing."

"And where do you think that our relationship has gone?"
she asked.

"So, I believe that we have learned how to relate well even if you, being from the big city, have had much more exposure and experience with life in the big world than I," said Cameron. "I am just some small-town kid compared to who you are."

"I'm nothing special, and you shouldn't compare yourself to anybody. You are you, and you have just as much potential as anyone else. I can see real growth in you since we first met, and you showed real courage when we first entered the light gate at the baseball park back in early September. You didn't freak out like so many have. That's when I knew that you had great potential," Sonja said. "Here it is only the end of October, and I believe that you can take the whole truth and begin to get prepared for what is coming."

"Now, there you go again. When you talk like that the tiny hairs stand up on the back of my neck. I start to imagine all kinds of strange things," said Cameron.

"I'm sorry for that and for the way that our relationship has gone so far, becoming so close. I hate to let you down, but we wouldn't have been and never can be closer than we have been throughout our season of knowing each other. I am here for a reason and a purpose, and that purpose is becoming realized soon," said Sonja.

"But …" began Cameron.

"Please, let me explain before you ask one more thing. I will answer any and all questions when I am finished, but I must tell you this. I believe that you have developed the ability to see beyond yourself to a wider concern for others, to see solutions for problems that even the most educated grownups would overlook. The benefits of solving problems and finding solutions should be realized and enjoyed by all, not just the ones struggling to find answers, the ones that caused the problems in the first place. We need to form a task group that works for the express collateral of humanity. If a solution like the ability to construct a water windmill from native materials rather than getting some huge, expensive, impersonal corporation to come in and build a large pumping station and then charges people that can't afford it for the water, that is what you need to be about.

"You have had growth in your life since I first met you and played catch in the ballpark venue. Remember the Town Woods and Snow Pond? The cave was quite an adventure." said Sonja.

“I could have gotten a lot more out of it, though,” said Cameron. “Couldn’t we go back to that venue and play through the other scenarios? They looked interesting.”

“There is little time for playing anymore,” she said. “I will continue. You do not see the change in you because it has been a natural growth process as we have been learning about what is important to develop. A sense of adventure and discovery come naturally for you and your friends, and that’s a plus. There were elements in the scenario at the zoo that threw you for a loop. However, working to get to a conclusion based only on what we see can have great drawbacks. I lost track of you while you were on the ship going to the processing station, but I was able to see your reaction and facial expression when you arrived.”

“How could that be? I never saw you there and didn’t see you again until I left the venue,” said Cameron.

“Remember, Cam, it was virtual. I could move around the matrix of the imaging, just like in the mall venue,” she explained. “I will never forget the look on your face when you understood that the people were being processed for food to feed the Vortak, something so opposite to what you were wanting to believe about them. It is almost like cheating to place a scenario before you that you couldn’t initiate a solution for, but we needed you to face the extinction of the human race as a real possibility. Being caged up wasn’t the real issue for the humans because they didn’t think that they were in any danger. I put it before you, Cam, that the cage you put yourself in when you sit down at your computer screen is the same: no sense of danger. But there is danger, and I think that you know that now. I am not making video games out to be evil, mind you. You know what I mean. Your brain receives a signal that we send which acts like an update to your mind software, like a video game console receiving updates for a game through the internet, only this is wireless technology for people, a kind of bio-Wi-Fi."

"I do know, and even though it wasn't real, and I knew that, it felt real and I felt helpless. Games don't usually do that and when they do, I shut them down and go away from it for a while. I still have bad dreams about that one," said Cameron. "But that's not saying much when I also have bad dreams about falling into Snow Pond."

"That's funny. So, Cam, you never thought that a trip to the zoo would show you how much you cared for the survival of the human race, did you? Rescue is a large part of why I am here," said Sonja. "In the scenario, the rescue of mankind was the only goal, having their entire world decimated, leaving nothing to show who they were or why they existed. That is really something. After the museum and the library, how much more worthy is mankind to be saved with all that you were shown in those venues?"

"For me, the mall and the picnic really showed how enjoyable it can be to simply provide for the needs of others and have your own needs met in the process. Now I sound like an infomercial spokesperson."

"Cameron?" Sonja said in a questioning tone. "I am Rapah, an off-world observer from Oros in the Topazoin realm."

It was so sudden that it took Cameron some time to respond. Shocked, he replied, "So your name is Rapah?"

"No, that is my race. Now it is out there, and I know that you have a thousand questions. Let me explain as best I can and then you can ask if you still have any," she began. "I am from a race of beings, Rapah, that exist outside of this dimension in one of twelve called the Topazoin realm. As hard as that is to believe, there is a planet called Oros that I call home. Topazoin can be interpreted as Zebulun which is one of the sons of Israel in your earth Bible and means 'a habitation.' You can consider it a habitation of spiritual messengers or angels. We have been observing many worlds in this realm and in the other eleven for centuries. The technology we employ is not something that you could market but more abilities afforded us by the Creator of the realms and worlds."

"So, you're not really from Boston. You're not even real?"

"Oh, I'm real enough, just not able to be 'real' here, Cam. Every time I get to this stage, I see how cruel it is. In every culture it is lying, no matter how I might try to justify it other than to know that we are trying with all that we know how to save worlds and cultures," she said. "Soon, you will have the second half to your key which will allow you to go and see your real father."

She started for the bus that had just pulled into the station. "I have to be going now, Cameron Adams. It was nice to have met you," she said.

Sonja turned back to face him as the doors of the bus opened and said, “Remember Cam, it’s a big world out there.”

There was an ethereal haze that materialized around her as she walked away to get on the bus, and as she stood there, she began to vanish into the air with people coming off and walking right through her. They must not have seen her as they walked right through her ghostly form, the whiffs of mist eddying around them. The doors to the bus closed with a sudden motion as it quickly pulled away.

‘A big world indeed.’ he thought as he stared off into the day.

Cameron stood there for a long time, contemplating the experience of falling in love with a virtual entity from another world. He felt that his life would have to change to accommodate the reality of what she had imparted to him with her visit. He knew that his friends would be on board with the directives that were given, and his future suddenly seemed very bright in a dark, disturbed world.

The next day at school, the homeroom had a Deja-Vu feeling to it for Cameron. He was hesitant to go, but his mom insisted. That morning he met up with Bill and Kevin and told them some of what his last moments with Sonja were like. They were changed by what they had gone through, and Cameron knew it. He also knew that it would take a long time to realize and understand the ramifications of it all. He wanted to include his friends every step of the way but he couldn't help missing Sonja even though she was an alien VR.

Their teacher for home room, Mrs. Dunnigan, began the class after the announcements by introducing another new student.

"Class, I want you to welcome Onda Salvati into our homeroom and community. She comes to us all the way from Albuquerque, New Mexico."

Cameron turned to Kevin and said, "That's her, the same girl that I saw get off the bus that Sonja was going to get on when she vanished. She was the first one that just walked right through her as she turned to vapor."

"You have got to be kidding me. What are the odds of that?" said Kevin.

At lunchtime Cameron's friends didn't have to force him to sit with Onda. He went right past them and over to the table she was at, sitting with some other girls he knew. Their eyes met, and Cameron knew that he wasn't butting in. He introduced himself to her. “Hi, my name is Cameron Adams. I’m glad to meet you, Onda. So, you’re from Albuquerque?”

“Yes, Cameron, nice to meet you,” she answered. “It’s quite a change, New Mexico to Massachusetts. I’m sure that I will get used to and like the seasons here. I’m already colder than I have ever been in New Mexico. My dad always referred to it as their tagline said, “Land of Enchantment” and he would add, “Bring your own enchantment.” Not that he minded living there, it’s just that he and my mom were originally from Michigan and missing the seasons and the snow. When this opening came along, he grabbed it quickly.”

“Isn’t It funny how people always want something different than what they are used to until they get it?” he said. “What could have possibly brought you here, Onda?”

“We have family here in Ware and in Boston. My dad just got a job with the Heritage Landscape Inventory program, and my mom is a stay-at-home mom with me and my two brothers and two sisters. One of them is my twin,” she said.

“What a coincidence. My dad works there as well. I only have one older brother, Chuck, but how is it having a twin?”

“That is odd,” she said. “It’s not bad. Not hard to get us mixed up: he is my brother, not my sister. I got you. You probably thought that it was my sister, right?”

“Well, it is the logical assumption. Salvati, that’s Italian, right?”

"Yes, that's right. My family, my grandparents, came from Casoria, Italy. It's north and a little east of Naples. I've been there several times over the years. A few that I have little or no memory of because I was so young," Onda replied. "Are you originally from here?"

"Yes, I'm from Ware ever, for ever, as we say. Kind of a local joke," Cameron returned. "I sure would like to talk to you some more, but we have to get back to class soon. Would you like to have pizza this weekend with some of my friends?"

"Sure, that would be fun. Can I meet you some Ware?"

"You're picking up on that local humor quickly. Sure, there's a restaurant called George's Astronaut Pizza House, 197 West Street; we go there a lot. We can meet there around 12:30 – 1:00 on Saturday. Would that be okay?"

"That will work. See you there, Cameron."

On his way to class, Cameron could not believe all of the coincidences about Sonja that seem to surround Onda. Her dad having the same job as his dad, both with an Italian last name, even her appearance was similar. She was tall, not quite as tall as Sonja, and her hair was black rather than dark brown, but it was as long, if not longer. And she was a bit more mature in places than the other girls in class. Not that that mattered, Cameron was just making comparison. Then there was the issue of Boston. Of course, Sonja had no connection with it, having no other earthly family. But why make it up if there wouldn't be a new student coming along with ties to it?

All that week, Cameron was distracted, anticipating the weekend when he could be with Onda. Even though they would be with Kevin, Bill and Peter, he was looking forward to it. Each day in class and just passing her in the halls made him feel good about how the whole situation with Sonja and the program went. He would sit with her at lunch, and they talked and got to know each other better. They had a lot more in common than Cameron could have guessed.

It was the longest week Cameron could remember but when Friday came around, he could hardly wait for the weekend.

Around noon the next day, Cameron was waiting outside the restaurant by his bike when Onda pulled up in a new Fiat 500 X. He wasn't sure that it was her until she got out.

"Is this your car?" he asked.

"Yes," she said. "I'm paying half and my parents are paying the other half. It's a deal that they make with all us kids. They pay half on any reasonable, large purchase if we agree to keep our grades up and chores done. So, it comes with an additional cost, but they say that it builds character and teaches responsibility. Anyway, I thought I would represent my heritage by getting something Italian."

"That sounds like a great philosophy. I'll have to tell my folks about it. Since there are only the two of us, it might be something that they would be willing to do," said Cameron.

As they were heading into the restaurant, Onda said, "I need to tell you something before we go any further." Cameron froze. What could it be? She continued, "I have been talking with some of the other students at school, mostly the girls, and do you know what you and your friends are called? Nerds and cave dwellers, that's what."

"Oh, yes, is that all. They say those things out of jealousy. We wear their taunts like badges of honor. It doesn't bother us too much; they have been doing it for a long time."

"Well, I just wanted you to know from the very beginning of our friendship that I don't have a problem with it, either," she said. "They don't know me at this school well enough yet, but in the weeks and months ahead, I will get the same names. Sooner, when they see me palling around with you guys."

"I don't know what to say," Cameron said. "This may sound strange, but I have never had such acceptance from a human female before. I can explain as we get to know each other better, but for now, I just hope that you are as accepting of my friends inside as well."

With that, they entered to find Bill, Kevin and Peter sitting at their usual round table in the corner with an extra-large pizza waiting for them.

Kevin held out two cups and said, "We took the liberty of ordering but didn't know what you wanted to drink." On the way over to the drink station, Cameron said, "They really are good friends and thoughtful. I usually get root beer, but sometimes I get Coke. Kevin knows that and when he knows what you prefer, he will have it sitting there waiting for you unless he comes late and then he expects you to have his Cherry Coke waiting for him. I guess that good friends know what you like to drink."

"That is really nerdy. I like Sprite," she said as they both started to laugh.

They went back to the table and Cameron started to introduce her, but they said, "We know her, Cameron. She knows who we are, right, Onda?" said Bill.

"Sure, Bill," and looking over to Peter, "and Peter and Kevin." They all sat down and started on the pizza talking as if they had known each other for a long time. From their favorite video games, movies and books, they found out that there was a lot of common ground. That is where it stopped though because Onda was from all over and had been all over the world whereas the Ware crowd had spent their entire lives in the same small town. That wasn't a problem, just a difference.

"This is quite a nerd fest in here," said Kevin as they got ready to divide up the leftover pizza and go their separate ways. It appeared as if the group was going to work. The bonding had begun.

"So, then Cameron, later tonight. Will we see you, or should I say, your avatar, in the game?" asked Bill.

"No, not tonight, guys. You should get Peter into the games, and then we will be a force to contend with," said Cameron.

"Okay then. Don't stay out too late, test on Monday," said Bill.

Cameron remembered seeing a bike rack on the back of Onda's car and asked if she would mind giving him a ride home.

"Sure, not a problem," she said.

"If you could, I want to show you something. There is a baseball field just a few blocks over from my house if you could go there first," Cameron asked.

They got the bike fastened and climbed into the car. On the way, Cameron wanted to tell her about Sonja and the training that she had given him. Likewise, Onda kind of sensed there was something that he wanted to explain. She took out her phone at one of the intersections on the way and showed him a text with a link to a website. It was from Sonja. The date was from almost a week ago, and it kind of unnerved Cameron.

"Are you real, Onda?"

"Yes, I am. I knew that you would wonder that eventually," she said. "My tutor in Albuquerque was called Harvey, and I was the only one that could see him. Have you ever seen the movie with Jimmy Stewart? Quite the sense of humor, wouldn't you say. You had it easy if all your friends could interact with Sonja. I had to keep from appearing crazy, talking to thin air and all that goes with it."

"Harvey, my Rapah from Oros in the Topazoin realm. An off-world observer," she said. "Kind of creepy when you step back and look at it. I was given clues that I would be working with someone when I got settled up here and then about a week ago, I received that message from Sonja. What do you say? Partners?" she asked as she took out a lavender-colored holalectrum.

"Is this the second half of the key she mentioned?" Cameron asked through choked tears of a mixture of emotions that he couldn't sort out. "Of all the crazy things she had me do and the places we went to, although they were created in a virtual dimension to teach me lessons, I fell in love with her," said Cameron. "That sounds crazy, doesn't it? I mean, she wasn't real. How pathetic is that?"

"Well, I believe that we can fall in love many different ways," said Onda. "We can even fall in love with an idea. With all that you have told me about your adventures, don't you think that it is an exciting prospect for our future? Think of it, an idea that might become our reality. I think that even being able to see your real dad again would be most exciting. Here, you can take it and give it back after you see him."

Cameron was caught off guard by Onda's pronouncement as he got a strange feeling about her. He read the message on her phone and it told Onda all about him and his training and that, 'Cam is in the highest one percentile score, so you will work well together.'

"She never did tell me what my final score was."

"Neither did my tutor, although I was also in the top one percentile. It seems that we were sort of made for each other," she concluded.

They pulled into Cameron's driveway and took the bike loose from the rack. Cameron turned to her and said, "I think that I will have to sleep on all of this that happened today. I hope that you had a good time with my dorky friends."

"It was real fun, Cam. We should get together often. See you at school tomorrow,"

"Yah, that would be good. Thank you for the ride home," Cameron said as he wheeled his bike up to the garage.

"She called me Cam, that takes the prize. How could all of this be orchestrated? It's not a coincidence."

Later that night, Cameron woke up around 2:30 and decided to take Sandy for a walk. They went to the ball field near his house. "This is where the last scenario played out, Sandy. Do you remember this place? It's where it all started. I thought you were a goner," he said. As he approached the field, he felt the gemstones in his pocket pulsing and getting hot. When he drew them out, the glow made the light gate shimmer and open for him to step through. He thought to himself, "Why am I able to do this? Am I really going to be a tutor for new recruits? Is my dad waiting in there?"

Sandy was visibly shaken up over the light gate. It must have brought back memories for her, but she followed Cameron through. Instantly, they were in the virtual ballfield with people in the stands, only their cheering was silent, and on the pitcher's mound was Cameron's real dad, Carmine. All of the players were milling around and acting as if there had just been a grand slam bases loaded home run hit. It was odd to see as it was all without sound.

His dad was sitting on a chair with a big smile on his round face. His beard was long and not trimmed up to his face like Cameron remembered it. His memories had begun to fade from when he was five-and-a-half-years-old but he did remember the beard.

Carmine called to him and motioned for him to come over. Walking over to the mound he thought that he noticed a redness to his complexion.

"I've been reminded of you often through the color red that was a part of my training sessions," Cameron said. "Carmine red."

"I'm so sorry that I had to leave you and your mom after my

accident. I know there is no way to make it up to you. It's very difficult for me to be here this way."

"She was right, you look just how I remember you other than the beard. It's like you never aged," Cameron said. "This is some technology."

Of course, Cameron knew that his dad could choose whatever avatar he wished to look like.

"It is, Cameron, but I am not able to move very far off of the pitcher's mound in this avatar," he said with sadness. "I don't understand why. I can see you and everyone back home though. I look in as often as I can, but I am pretty busy with the program."

"I don't know why she was so cryptic about where I could see you, but this is kind of an obvious place. I remember playing catch with you here. You bought me my first baseball glove," said Cameron.

"She knew that you would come here, and after you met Onda she knew that Onda would give you her gemstone, you would have both of them which opens this gate to me," Carmine explained. "If you had come with only your own holalectrum, it would have only opened the ballfield scenario. You can come here to see me whenever you want, but I can only be active when I'm not busy and then it can only be for about thirty minutes. Cameron, I'm so sorry that it happened this way, but I was busted up pretty bad in the accident.

“I consider myself as being one of the Rapah, and we have collected solutions to numerous global issue problems from many worlds that have been visited. Some worked to solve their own issues, and some would have worked if the population could have expanded their thinking to include alternative courses of action.”

“Why can’t the solutions just be given out to us, say, in a book of world solutions?” asked Cameron. “Don’t you think that we could figure it out?”

“We can’t just give it all to earth, and some things we won’t. Man’s pride wouldn’t allow some otherworldly source to come in and change things.” He straightened up and looked more serious as he continued, “Mankind has to be made to see the solutions coming from themselves, and some of the solutions are based on how man sees his relationship to other men and races. Talk about pride and prejudice, Earth wrote the book on that.”

Cameron laughed and thought to himself how good it would have been to have grown up with him even if he had to endure his dad jokes.

“Good, lasting solutions that work have to come from the people of earth. It gives them credibility and ownership, and some day, hopefully, the Rapah may get some credit for having helped. That is what I am counting on, that there will be a ‘someday’ for earth,” he said with severity in his voice. “With a little help from technologies that come from other worlds, given as hints to begin the creative juices flowing, and with the right motives, they will win out rather than just plopping down some alien what-cha-ma-call-it solutions in a box. The principles and scientific understanding and explanations will need to come from mankind in order for them to embrace it as their own."

"I keep hearing about these problems, and I can't recall how bad off the world is. What are some of these so-called problems that must be addressed? What threatens the survival of the human race?"

"Well, son, I have been giving that a lot of thought over the years, and I have come to the conclusion that if the basic needs of mankind are met, there is no limit to what they can accomplish," he began.

"Okay, I've heard this before from Sonja. The security and significance talk," Cameron said with derision.

"No, but that is what comes into play after these things have been properly taken care of. Namely, food, water and clothing. I know that it sounds simple, but it is an almost insurmountable task to ensure that every man, woman and child in the world has good, clean water to drink; healthy, nutritional food to eat; and the proper clothing for their environments. After that they can get to work on the rest of the issues that need their attention. Education, employment, crime, energy, pollution, unstable economies, drugs, threats of terrorisms like nuclear, chemical and genocide, disease, wars, human trafficking, abortion, unloved people, selfishness and the list goes on and on.

"Some of these things are not even seen as problems by vast majorities, so how do you offer a solution to what seems to not be a problem? Most of these issues will take care of themselves when the underlying cause is addressed. That is where the tutors come in. Last I knew, we had 7,859 active trainers in the project that was begun in 1976."

"Sonja told me that you were one of the original twelve in the program. How could you go through the scenarios in such bad physical condition?" Cameron asked.

"It wasn't video games that I learned from back then, and it wasn't easy for me even sitting at a desk," he replied. "I believe that we can put forth an effort that can bring the world out of a tailspin of destruction if we are committed to doing our part. What do you say, son?"

"Knowing that you are here for me and that I can come and see you anytime I need to will make it a lot easier, but I have school and friends and mom, Chuck and Carmine too. Will they be included in the covertness of what is going on?" said Cameron.

"We have set up a network of cells all around the globe able to access tech and information on what is going on in the different regions for needs and progress on cultural assimilation of world tech. There is a link on your real time computer for accessing the network and identifying your rank by your holalectrum. It's not just for training anymore," As the projection of his avatar began to flicker, Carmine said, "Yes, we will include them as time goes on. I must be going soon; the transmission is becoming too weak to sustain the image. I love you, son."

As it continued to weaken, the audio went out as well and just before his dad went dark, he caught a glimpse of what he must have actually looked like. His body was grossly deformed, and he was reclining in a special chair that appeared to be made just for him.

"Well, Sandy, this puts an entirely new light on things. What say we go home, hay boy?"

The End

www.ingramcontent.com/pod-product-compliance
Lightning Source LLC
Chambersburg PA
CBHW060612310726
48982CB00003B/535

* 9 7 8 1 9 6 0 1 0 1 0 1 3 *